MW01115240

ABOUT THE AUTHOR

David Parks has lived almost all of his life in Weston, West Virginia. He is the youngest of four children born to Don and Carole Parks. David graduated from Lewis County High School, graduated from Glenville State College with his Bachelors Degree and Graduated from the University of Cincinnati with his Master's Degree.

David has been married since 1989 to Lisa and has two wonderful daughters, Daphne and Deidre.

This is David's second book, his first book is:

"The Mysteries of Dallback Ridge"

ACKNOWLEDGEMENTS

I would like to thank my family and friends for their help and support in my quest to write this book. I would also like to thank my friends who helped me by giving advice and feedback.

This story is purely fiction and any similarities with real events are truly coincidental.

This story is set at the Trans-Allegheny Lunatic Asylum which is a real historical facility located in Weston, West Virginia. It is a true American Historical site and if you have never been there, I would recommend you experience it. I got the following information from the Internet:

"Welcome to the Trans-Allegheny Lunatic Asylum. Formerly known as the Weston State Hospital, this West Virginia facility served as a sanctuary for the mentally ill in the mid-1800's. The history of the building holds fascinating stories of Civil War tales, a gold robbery, the "curative" effects of architecture, and the efforts of determined individuals to help better the lives of the mentally ill. Tour this nationally recognized landmark and see how it left a lasting impression on local and national history. Daily heritage tours are available for both small and large groups."

For more information you can look up the facility on the Internet or go to Weston, West Virginia for a tour.

Night Terrors

By: David S. Parks

Night Terrors

Chapter One

Joey

"Help Mom!" A young boy's screams echoed through the darkness.

"Joey, are you all right?" A female's voice quickly responds as footsteps pound on the floor drawing closer and the light came on in the hallway.

"Mom, I'm alright I just had a bad dream," Joey replied as his mother, Sue, came running into his bedroom.

Sue turned on the light and sat down on the bed beside him. She gently takes his hand, "Honey, this is the third nightmare this week. Is it the same nightmare?"

"Yeah, in the same building," Joey said.

"Why can't you just put that place out of your mind?" Sue insisted.

"I don't know, I feel like I belong there or something," Joey said.

"Joey, you are nine years old. How could you have a connection with a place you have never been?" Sue asked.

"I don't know, but I can see myself in the building in every nightmare. The spirits are calling me to come to it." Joey explained.

"What do you mean 'spirits are calling you?'" Sue asked.

"In my nightmares there are spirits standing in the hallways and I go with them. They are talking to me, they take me places in the big building. I just follow them and we do things, they're not all bad." Joey said.

Sue got goose bumps on her arms and chills from the fear of imagining what Joey was describing.

"OK that's enough. Now lay down and get some rest." Sue said as she pulled the covers up onto Joey.

"Good night, Mom. I love you," Joey told her.

"I love you, too, baby," Sue replied as she stood and walked out of Joey's bedroom.

"Is he OK?" Joey's dad, Jim, asked.

"He will be OK, he's going back to sleep," Sue replied.

"What happened?" Jim asked.

"It's that building again, he's never even been there but still has nightmares about it," Sue replied.

"How could he dream it if he has never been there?" Jim asked.

"When I was a little girl I used to have bad dreams, but none as specific as his. Every time he starts describing the building to me, I just can't imagine where it would be," Sue said.

"Have you ever told him stories that would make him think about a building or someplace like he describes?" Jim asked.

"I have never talked about going anywhere. I even looked on the Internet and can't find a picture of any building like he was describing," Sue replied.

"I just don't get it then. Do you think he is just doing it for attention?" Jim asked.

"I don't know. All I know is he is getting less sleep than ever. Maybe we should consider taking him to a psychiatrist," Sue continued as she turned out the lights.

Sue woke the next morning and got Joey off to school as normal. She then became focused on finding a local psychiatrist and making an appointment for Joey to talk to them.

"Mom, I'm home," Joey yells walking in the door.

"I'm in the kitchen," Sue replies.

"I'm hungry," Joey said.

"I put some cookies on the counter and there is a juice box beside them," Sue said.

Joey goes to the counter and quickly stuffs a cookie in his mouth as he wrestles to pull the straw out of the wrapper of the juice box.

"Joey?" Sue hesitantly speaks to Joey from the kitchen.

"Yeah, mom," Joey replies.

"You know how you sometimes have those bad dreams at night?" Sue asked.

"Yeah," Joey responded.

"There is someone I would like you to talk to, about your dreams," Sue said.

"Who?" Joey curiously asked.

"He's like a doctor, a doctor who listens to your problems." Sue replied.

"OK," Joey said without hesitation. "When?"

"I don't know honey, I will make an appointment and let you know," Sue said.

Sue was relieved that Joey was willing to talk to someone about his nightmares. She was also afraid to hear what may result from the visit. Sue looked through the phone book and found a psychiatrist who had been in practice just over a year. Sue felt that this doctor would have a fresh mind and would be a good fit for Joey. Sue called the doctor's office and made an appointment for Joey for the following week.

The following week Sue pulled up in front of Deerfield Junior High School and waited for Joey to come out.

"Hey mom," Joey yells as he heads down the sidewalk.

"Hey honey, how was school?" Sue asked.

"It was good. I have a spelling test tomorrow," Joey answered.

"You'll do fine. You just have to study tonight," Sue said.

"I know," Joey affirmed.

"Do you remember where we are going today?" Sue asked.

"Yeah, we are going to the talking doctor," Joey replied.

"That's right, we are going to see the talking doctor," Sue said.

"What's his name?" Joey asked.

"His name is Dr. Robert," Sue said.

"Dr. Robert? That sounds weird," Joey replied.

"He is a very nice man, you will like him," Sue reassured him as she pulled in Dr. Robert's parking lot.

"I'm a little afraid," Joey said.

"You have no reason to be afraid, I will be right there with you," Sue said as she parked the car.

They got out of the car and walked into Dr. Robert's office.

"May I help you?" the receptionist asked.

"We have an appointment to see Dr. Robert," Sue said.

"Well, you must be Joey?" The receptionist asked, smiling at Joey.

"Yeah, I'm Joey," he replied.

"You look like a big boy, are you excited to meet with Dr. Robert today?" the receptionist asked.

"No, I'm kind of scared," Joey admitted.

"You don't need to be afraid, you will like Dr Robert," the receptionist tried to reassure Joey.

"Ma'am, you need to fill out this form and when we call your name bring it back to me," the receptionist said to Sue as she handed her a clipboard.

"Joey?" A young woman walked out of a door on the opposite side of the waiting room.

"Do you want me to go with you?" Sue asked.

"No mom, I am a big boy and I want to go alone," Joey said as he got up and walked toward the woman.

"Hello Joey, follow me," the woman said as she headed down the hallway.

"OK," Joey said, walking behind her.

"Right in here," the woman said entering a room that appeared to be an office. There was a desk back towards the back wall of the room with a couch and two chairs sitting in the middle of the room.

"If you want to have a seat, the doctor will be here in a couple minutes," the woman said.

"Do I have to lay down?" Joey asked.

"No, only if you want to," she replied.

"I think I'll sit in this chair," Joey said as he sat down in one of the chairs.

"That's fine," the woman said as she left the room.

Joey sat quietly for a couple minutes, until a middle aged man walked in wearing black pants and a white turtleneck shirt.

"Joey? I'm Dr. Robert," the man said as he walked into the room and sat in the empty chair.

"Hello," Joey said, watching Dr. Robert enter the room.

"Did your mom tell you why you are here?" Dr. Robert asked.

"My bad dreams?" Joey answered.

"That's right, I just want to talk about your dreams, if that's OK with you?" Dr. Robert asked.

"I guess it's OK," Joey answered.

"If you don't want to talk about your dreams, we can talk about something else," Dr. Robert said.

"No, we can talk about my dreams," Joey replied in a confident tone.

"Your mom told me that you dream the same dream every night?" Dr. Robert asked.

"No," Joey replied.

"What do you dream?" Dr. Robert continued.

"I dream about the same place every night," Joey said.

"Oh, the same place, where do you dream you are?" Dr. Robert asked.

"I dream I'm in an old building that is very big," Joey replied.

"Do you know where the building is?" Dr. Robert asked.

"No, it's a big and very old building," Joey stated again.

"Can you describe the building for me?" Dr. Robert asked.

"It is a big stone building with a white clock on top that goes up to the sky in a point," Joey said.

"Can you see anything else around it?" Dr. Robert asked.

"No, just the building," Joey replied.

"How often do you dream about the building?" Dr. Robert asked.

"I don't know, but I don't dream about anything else but that building," Joey explained.

"What happens in your dreams?" Dr. Robert asked.

"Different things. I walk in the front door and go to different places in the building. Someone meets me at the door and takes me to where they live in the building and then we do different things. Sometimes the people get mad and yell at me and I think they want to hurt me, but most of the time the people are nice to me," Joey said.

"What do they want to talk about?" Dr. Robert asked.

"They are mostly lonely and just want to talk about where they came from, and then we play and stuff," Joey said.

"In your dreams, are the people real or are they ghosts?" Dr. Robert asked.

"They are real people, I can't see through them or anything," Joey said. "Do you think I'm crazy?"

"No, you're not crazy. I just want to help you figure out why you keep having these dreams," Dr. Robert explained.

"Why do I have the dreams?" Joey asked, echoing Dr. Robert.

"I don't know yet. Why don't we do a little experiment?" Dr. Robert said, walking over to his desk. "Come over here to my desk for me."

"OK," Joey said as he walked over and sat down in the chair by Dr. Robert's desk.

"Here are some blank sheets of paper. Why don't you draw me a picture of something from your dreams," Dr. Robert said.

"I can't draw very well," Joey said.

"It's OK, just do the best you can," Dr. Robert explained.

Joey picked up a pencil and held it to the paper like he was getting ready to begin to write, but he stopped as if he had froze.

"Are you OK, Joey?" Dr. Robert asked, noticing he was motionless.

"I don't want you to watch. I'm not good at drawing pictures," Joey explained.

"I'll tell you what, I have a couple things to do in the other room. If you don't mind sitting alone for a couple minutes, I'll go and will be back soon," Dr. Robert said.

"I'll be OK, you can go," Joey said.

Dr. Robert stood up and walked out the door, leaving Joey at the desk with a pencil and paper. After the door shut, Joey picked up the pencil and stared at blank sheet of paper for a few seconds. He slowly lifted his head and his eyes rolled back into his head. He leveled his head and the whites of his eyes stared straight ahead while his hand began drawing a picture. His hand moved wildly across the paper in an almost random pattern, and slowly the picture started to take form. Without warning, he quickly moved the page to the side and began drawing on the next sheet. He continued for several minutes until he collapsed on the desk as if he had suddenly fallen asleep.

"OK, let's see how we are doing," Dr. Robert said entering the room. "Joey, are you OK?"

"What?" Joey said lifting his head. "I must have fallen asleep. I'm sorry Dr. Robert."

Dr. Robert looked at an array of pictures on the desk and asked, "Who drew these pictures?"

"I don't know. I fell asleep," Joey said.

Dr. Robert knew that no one had been in the room with Joey. But he felt Joey had been pushed enough for the day so he decided to let him leave and then analyze the drawings.

Dr. Robert sat down in his chair and looked over at Joey and asked, "Did you have a pretty good time today?"

"It wasn't too bad," Joey replied.

"Would you be interested in coming back another day?" Dr. Robert asked.

"I guess... If my mom lets me," Joey replied.

"OK, are you ready to go?" Dr. Robert asked.

"Yeah," Joey said, standing up and walking toward the door.

Dr. Robert walked behind Joey as he went into the waiting room where Sue was waiting.

"Hey buddy, are you done?" Sue asked Joey.

"Yeah," Joey replied.

"I would like to meet with Joey again next week if that's OK with you?" Dr. Robert asked Sue.

"What do you think?" Sue said looking at Joey.

"I don't care. It's OK with me," Joey said.

"OK then, I will see you next week," Dr. Robert said.

"Bye Dr. Robert," Joey said as he and his mom walked out the door.

Dr. Robert returned to his office and sat down at his desk. He straightened the stack of pictures that Joey had drawn and began looking at them one at a time. The first picture was the entrance of the building from the outside, the front doors were open and the foyer was drawn in great detail. Looking through the pictures, Dr. Robert realized that the drawings were detailed views of the inside of an old building in different locations. Some of the drawings showed markings on doors and some showed detailed equipment. But it was clear that they were all deep inside the building.

Chapter Two

Finding the Building

Dr. Robert began investigating all the buildings in the area and could not find one like the one Joey had described in his dreams and in his drawings. He sat in front of the computer for hours, using key words to try to locate the mysterious building with no result. He decided to take a break from the search and began looking at the drawings again. He spent several minutes closely analyzing each drawing, when he noticed the word 'TALA'. He looked up the word in his dictionary and found it did not exist. He went back to the computer and typed in TALA in the search engine and the first response was Trans-Allegheny Lunatic Asylum in Weston, West Virginia, which was about thirty miles from his office. Investigating the asylum he found that the construction of the asylum started in 1858, but it did not actually house patients until 1864, due to delays created as a result of the Civil War. The building is the largest hand cut stone building in the United States and was closed to patients in 1994. It appeared after the asylum was closed, it was sold on the courthouse steps to the highest bidder in 2007. Dr. Robert decided to contact the new owners to find out if there were any connection between Joey and the asylum.

"Trans-Allegheny Lunatic Asylum, this is Rebecca. How may I help you?" a female voice answered the phone.

"Hello, this is Dr. Robert and I am a psychiatrist working in Deerfield, West Virginia. I am about thirty miles north of Weston and I have some questions about the asylum. I was hoping you could help me." Dr. Robert explained.

"Sure, how can I help?" Rebecca answered.

"I was wondering if the asylum is open for tours, or if there's a way I can see inside of the asylum?" Dr. Robert asked.

"Yes, we have tours seven days a week. But if you would like to come down and meet with me, I can give you a personal tour," Rebecca offered.

"That would be great. Can I run down this afternoon?" Dr. Robert said.

"Sure, can you be here around two?" Rebecca asked.

"Two would be great," Dr. Robert replied.

Dr. Robert hung up the phone and was excited about the cooperation he was getting from Rebecca. He gathered the drawings, put them in his brief case and headed out of the office. He drove to Weston early and decided to drive around the asylum to get a feel for the building before his meeting. He followed the directions, which he downloaded from the Internet, which led him directly to the front gate of the old asylum. Looking at the building it was an amazing sight, and he recalled reading that the structure was over 455,000 square feet. The appearance was over whelming, with the main building stretching almost a half mile wide, and a huge white clock tower engulfing the middle top of the building. The yard in front of the building was green and well maintained with a blacktop driveway leading to the entrance. Dr. Robert pulled to the main entrance and parked with his passenger window rolled down. He opened his briefcase and pulled out the picture of the front of the asylum that Joey had drawn and was amazed at the exactness of the drawing.

A loud noise broke Dr. Roberts' concentration as someone pounded on his window, startling him. Dr. Robert looked up to see a slender woman in her early thirties standing outside his window dressed in black slacks with a red blouse.

"Dr. Robert?" A woman yelled through the window.

Dr. Robert rolled down his window and asked, "Rebecca?"

"Yes, you can park over there," she said as she pointed to a small parking lot.

Dr. Robert parked his car, picked up his briefcase and walked back to where Rebecca was standing.

"Hello, it's nice to meet you," Dr. Robert said.

"Nice to meet you. Are you ready for your tour?" Rebecca asked.

"That would be great," Dr. Robert answered. "Do you offer this type of tour to everyone?"

"No, but we go out of our way for psychiatrists and basically anyone in the medical field," Rebecca said.

"I appreciate that," Dr. Robert replied.

"Do you want to know the history of the asylum, or do you just want to walk through the building?" Rebecca asked.

"I looked up the information on the Internet, but if I have any questions I will ask," Dr. Robert replied.

"OK, this is the front entrance. All patients who came in the building came through this entrance," Rebecca said, walking through the double doors into the building.

Entering the building, Dr. Robert recalled that Joey had drawn a large circular counter area in the middle of the corridor, and there was no counter in the area. This lessened the validity of the drawings.

"Walking into the building, the patients used to see the doctor for their initial physical exam in the first door on the left, and when the hospital first opened there was a unique circular counter in this area," Rebecca said, pointing at the floor in the middle of the corridor.

"Wow!" Dr. Robert had a shocked look on his face as she continued to describe the counter and it was identical to the description that Joey had drawn.

"What's wrong Dr. Robert?" Rebecca asked.

"Oh, I'm sorry. I was thinking out loud. What were you saying?" Dr. Robert said.

"If you will follow me, we'll go into the different sections of the asylum, and I'll be able to tell you about what they did in each section," Rebecca said.

Systematically Rebecca led Dr. Robert into the various areas of the asylum starting on the first floor, then onto the second and finishing on the third floor. Dr. Robert identified most areas in relation to the pictures that Joey had drawn, but there were two pictures that he could not identify. Dr. Robert decided to try to ask

Rebecca about the areas without divulging any information about the pictures.

"Is there a basement in this building?" Dr. Robert asked.

"Yes there is but we rarely go there. It is full of old equipment and cleaning supplies and all kinds of things like that," Rebecca said.

"Have you ever been in the basement?" Dr. Robert asked.

"I have, but only a couple of times, and it's a mess," Rebecca replied.

"Can I see the basement?" Dr. Robert asked.

"Sure, but if you don't mind, I'll let Charlie, our maintenance man, take you and show you the basement," Rebecca said.

"That will be fine," Dr. Robert replied.

Rebecca pulls a two way radio from her belt and says, "Charlie?"

After a few seconds the radio replied, "Go ahead Rebecca."

"Charlie, can you come meet me at the front entrance?" Rebecca asked.

"I'll be there in a couple minutes," Charlie replied.

"If there is nothing more I can help you with, I'll leave you for Charlie," Rebecca said.

Dr. Robert stood in the front foyer area, waiting for Charlie. He looked around the foyer. The door of the front office was slightly cracked open, and Dr. Robert moved towards the door. Suddenly a black figure moved quickly across the door opening, startling Dr.

Robert. He decided to step closer to see what was inside the door, slowly stepping closer and sticking his head towards the crack.

"Hey!" a male's voice echoed through the hall, making Dr. Robert jump.

"Hey," Dr Robert said turning around to see a man in his mid fifties wearing a khaki type uniform, a ball cap and sporting a full beard and mustache.

"I'm Charlie. Rebecca told me to meet you here and show you anywhere in the asylum you want to look," Charlie said.

"I'm Dr. Robert. I was wondering if you could show me through the basement?" Dr. Robert asked.

"There's nothing down there but junk," Charlie explained.

"I was told by someone about a doorway that led back into a tunnel," Dr. Robert said.

"There's no tunnel in this place, someone was pulling your leg," Charlie said.

"Will you show me down in the basement anyway?" Dr. Robert asked.

"Rebecca's the boss. If she said you can go down there, then you can go down there," Charlie said as he began walking down the hallway.

"How long have you worked here?" Dr. Robert asked.

"I worked here when it was full," Charlie said.

"I bet you could tell some stories about the people that have come through here," Dr. Robert asked.

"Buddy, I have seen some things that would make the hair stand up on your toes," Charlie said.

"Would you be interested in telling me any of those stories?" Dr. Robert asked.

"No, not really," Charlie said.

"OK," Dr. Robert said in a surprised tone.

"Right down here, watch your steps," Charlie said as he headed down a set of stairs.

"It's kind of dark down here," Dr. Robert said.

"Just stay behind me and you'll be OK," Charlie said as he continued to walk down the stairs. The light slowly began to vanish the further they travelled down the stairs.

"Are there any lights down here?" Dr. Robert asked.

"Yeah, but we ain't got to the switch yet," Charlie replied. "Stop right there,"

Charlie continued down a couple stairs and then navigated his way through the darkness and flipped on the lights. There was a small foyer area at the bottom of the stairs with a large wooden door that led into the basement. Charlie pulled hard on the door, and it slowly dragged open across the floor. Charlie stepped into the next room where he turned the light on as he entered.

"It's not very bright down here, is it?" Dr. Robert asked.

"No, there aren't any windows down here and only one light bulb in each room," Charlie said.

Looking around the room, Dr. Robert noticed an array of old wicker wheel chairs and wooden equipment piled against the walls.

"Wow, this is like a blast from the past. I haven't seen some of this stuff except for in a book," Dr. Robert said, walking around the room.

"Yeah, bunch of junk, if you ask me," Charlie said.

"Where does this door go?" Dr. Robert asked, looking at a large wooden door.

"We can go in there, it's just a maze of rooms and hallways that will eventually lead to the other end of the building," Charlie said.

"Would you mind showing me? I am looking for an old double wooden door system with an elaborate fancy wooden trim," Dr. Robert explained.

"I remember seeing an entrance like that, but it leads into a small broom closet," Charlie said.

"Can we go there?" Dr. Robert asked.

"Sure, it's just right over here," Charlie said walking ahead of Dr. Robert.

After navigating through several rooms with poorly lit passages, Charlie walked into a room that had plywood lying against one wall.

"Help me move this plywood," Charlie said as he grabbed the edge of one of the pieces. Dr. Robert grabbed the edge of the plywood and helped Charlie lift it away from the wall and onto another wall. Charlie grabbed another piece and Dr. Robert followed his lead and grabbed it with him. After moving four sheets of plywood, the wall became exposed to display a fancy wooden trim that held a double-door system just as Dr. Robert explained. Dr. Robert stood and stared in amazement at the doors, amazed at how exact the doors were to the ones in Joey's drawing.

"Want to see inside?" Charlie asked.

"Absolutely," Dr. Robert said, remembering that Joey had drawn the doors with a long tunnel behind them.

Charlie grabbed the handle of the door and pulled hard due to the moisture in the basement warping it.

"There we go," Charlie said when he finally got the door opened all the way. "Let me get the light."

Behind the door was a room that spanned close to ten feet wide and twelve feet deep, the walls had a variety of old brooms, mops, desks, and other old office supplies that appeared to have been stored and long forgotten. Dr. Robert walked around the room, looking through the dust and spider webs at the old supplies left behind.

"Is this the only door like this?" Dr. Robert asked.

"Yeah, I have been every place in this facility, and this is the only large double door like this," Charlie replied.

"I was once told that there was a tunnel in this place, is that true?" Dr. Robert asked.

"That's just rumors and stories. If there is a tunnel in this place I ain't never seen it," Charlie said.

"OK, I think I have seen enough," Dr. Robert said as he headed toward the door.

Charlie and Dr. Robert retraced their steps back out of the basement and up the stairs to the first floor.

"This place feels kind of spooky, do you ever get that feeling?" Dr. Robert said.

"Every once in a while but I just focus on my work and don't pay no attention to anything else. There are several people who tell stories about stuff that happened, but I really don't pay no attention to them," Charlie said.

"What do you mean... 'you don't pay attention'?" Dr. Robert asked.

"I just ignore the people who say they saw things, and if I see something, I just keep it to myself and do my job," Charlie replied.

"How do you just ignore strange things that happen around you?" Dr. Robert asked.

"Mister, I live a simple life. I have raised three kids by working here and don't plan on making no waves. I can retire in two years, so I am not saying a word about anything," Charlie said as they reached the main entrance.

"Thank you for your time," Dr. Robert said as he stepped out the door, realizing that Charlie did not want to get involved in anything going on in the asylum.

Dr. Robert returned to his office and laid Joey's drawings out on his table. He looked at the pictures one at a time, comparing each drawing with what he remembered seeing in the asylum. Each picture was meticulously drawn, and Dr. Robert tried to find flaws in each drawing. While laying each drawing to the side after looking at it Dr. Robert noticed that there were names written on the back of each drawing. Dr. Robert got a piece of paper and began listing the pictures with the corresponding names out from it. The drawing that indicated the front entrance did not have a name on it, but the drawing of the south corridor had "Eli" written on the back, the examination room drawing had "Patrick" written on the back, the drawing of the tunnel indicated "Sharon" on the back, and the auditorium had "Don" written on the back of it. Dr. Robert walked to his desk and sat down thinking about how he could address the drawings with Joey. He realized that any number of questions could scare Joey and he could shut down and stop talking. He picked up the phone and dialed Joey's number.

"Hello?" Sue answered.

"Sue, this is Dr. Robert. Do you have a minute to talk?" Dr. Robert asked.

"Why? Is something wrong?" Sue asked.

"No, I was just wondering how Joey's doing?" Dr. Robert asked.

"He's doing fine, he hasn't had a dream in the last few nights," Sue said.

"I was just wondering if it would be OK if Joey came back to see me one day," Dr. Robert said.

"I don't know. He really has not had any nightmares since he was there," Sue said.

"Well," Dr. Robert paused, "he confided a great deal in me, and I really would like to follow up on a couple things."

"I don't suppose it would hurt for him to come back," Sue said.

"That would be great. How soon can he come in?" Dr. Robert asked.

"We are free about any evening after school," Sue advised.

"Great, can you come in after school tomorrow evening?" Dr. Robert asked.

"Yeah, that shouldn't be a problem," Sue replied.

"OK, I will see you around four." Dr. Robert asked.

Chapter Three

Talking about the Dreams

The following day Dr. Robert had a limited client list. In between his appointments, he focused on Joey's drawings, anxiously awaiting Joey's arrival and making a list of questions that he wanted to ask. Just before four o'clock, Joey and his mother walked in the front entrance of the doctor's office.

"Hey Joey, how are you doing today?" Dr. Robert anxiously asked.

"OK, how are you Dr. Robert?" Joey replied in a happy tone.

"I'm doing great. Joey, before we get started, would you mind if I spoke to your mother for a minute?" Dr. Robert asked.

"No," Joey answered.

"Sue, would you mind coming back with me for a minute?" Dr. Robert asked.

"No, I don't mind," Sue said.

Dr. Robert led Sue to the back office, "Please have a seat."

"What's going on?" Sue sounded concerned.

"Well, I found the building that Joey keeps dreaming about," Dr. Robert said.

"Where?" Sue asked excitedly.

"It's called the Trans-Allegheny Lunatic Asylum and it's in Weston. It's an old asylum for mentally impaired and insane people that closed many years ago. Has Joey ever been there?" Dr. Robert asked.

"To a crazy house, no." Sue said defensively.

"It's not an asylum now, it's a tourist attraction," Dr. Robert explained.

"No, I know where Weston is, but I don't think Joey has ever been there," Sue said.

"Well, now that we know the place we are dealing with, we need to try to figure out the problem," Dr. Robert assured Sue.

"Is there anything I can do?" Sue offered.

"No, I went to the asylum and am going to try to get Joey to explain some of the things that are going on and maybe I can get him to stop having the nightmares," Dr. Robert said.

Dr. Robert stood and walked toward the door, "Thanks for your time."

"Thank you," Sue replied, walking back toward the waiting room.

"Are you ready to come on back?" Dr. Robert asked as he opened the door. "Do you remember what room you were in last time?"

"Sure, this one," Joey said, stopping at a closed door.

"That's right. You can go on in," Dr. Robert said.

Joey opened the door and went into the office, and Dr. Robert walked in behind him. Joey stopped right inside the door, and Dr. Robert walked around him and sat down behind his desk.

"I talked to your mom, and she told me that you have stopped having the bad dreams?" Dr. Robert asked.

"No," Joey said in a simple tone.

"No?" Dr. Robert said, looking for clarification.

"No, I just don't tell my mom when I have them," Joey said.

"Why don't you tell your mom?" Dr. Robert asked.

"She gets worried when I tell her about my dreams. I just don't like it when she worries," Joey said.

"Can I ask you some questions about your dreams?" Dr. Robert asked.

"Yeah," Joey said as he walked to the chair across the desk from Dr. Robert and sat down.

Dr Robert looked at his notes, "You told me last time that you meet people when you go to the building, is that right?"

"Yeah," Joey replied.

"Can you tell me name of one of the people you have met?" Dr. Robert asked.

"Yeah," Joey answered.

Dr. Robert hesitated for a few seconds waiting for Joey to respond and then said, "OK, tell me one name."

"Patrick," Joey said, quietly looking down at the floor.

"Patrick, can you describe what Patrick looks like?" Dr. Robert asked.

"He's tall and wears a dress," Joey said.

"OK, how tall is he? Is he as tall as me?" Dr. Robert said, standing up to give Joey a visual comparison.

"He's a little taller than you," Joey said, looking up at Dr. Robert.

"OK, we'll say about six feet tall. What kind of dress does he wear?" Dr. Robert asked.

"It's white and it has strings on the back," Joey explained.

"It has fringes hanging down from the bottom?" Dr. Robert asked.

"No, you hook it together by the strings," Joey explained.

"Oh... a hospital gown," Dr. Robert figuring out what Joey was trying to say.

"I guess," Joey replied, not really knowing what a hospital gown was.

"How old is Patrick?" Dr. Robert asked.

"He said he was thirty, but his face looks younger than his body," Joey explained.

"What do you mean?" Dr. Robert continued.

"He just looks and plays like a little kid, but his body is old," Joey said.

"OK, where do you meet Patrick?" Dr. Robert asked, realizing Patrick was probably a mentally retarded person.

"I meet everyone at the door, and then we go to where they want to go in the building," Joey explained.

"I see, do you meet someone different every time your dream takes you there?" Dr Robert asked.

"No, I mostly meet four people, but Patrick is my favorite," Joey said.

"Why is Patrick your favorite?" Dr. Robert asked.

"We play when I go there with him," Joey said.

"What do you play when you meet Patrick?" Dr. Robert asked.

"Mostly jacks, but sometimes hopscotch," Joey answered.

"Who wins?" Dr. Robert asked, trying to keep Joey interested.

"I do most of the time," Joey said smiling.

"What happens when your dream ends?" Dr. Robert asked.

"I go back out the front door and wake up or I just wake up," Joey replied.

"Do you ever see more than one person?" Dr. Robert asked.

"No, just the person that meets me at the door," Joey shrugged.

"Where do you and Patrick go when you get there?" Dr. Robert asked.

"We go in the front door and turn right and go to the last room on the right," Joey explained.

"What is in the room?" Dr. Robert asked.

"It has a big bed and all kinds of doctor stuff in there," Joey said.

"What do you mean 'doctor stuff'?" Dr. Robert asked.

"Stuff to look in your ears, eyes - stuff like that," Joey said.

"Was it like an examination room?" Dr. Robert asked.

"I guess," Joey replied.

"Can I show you a drawing?" Dr. Robert asked.

"Sure," Joey replied.

Dr. Robert pulled the drawing which had "Patrick" written on the back and laid it on the desk in front of Joey.

"That's it! That's the room!" Joey said excitedly.

"Is this where you and Patrick always play?" Dr. Robert asked.

"Yeah, we stay in that room all the time," Joey replied.

"Do you know why you go to that room?" Dr. Robert asked.

"No, we just go to that room every time," Joey said.

"OK, tell me about another person you meet at the building," Dr. Robert said.

"Patrick is my favorite, but next would probably be Don," Joey said.

"Where do you meet Don?" Dr. Robert asked.

"I meet everyone at the door," Joey gave Dr. Robert a frustrated glare for making him repeat his answers.

"That's right, I'm sorry I forgot you said that," Dr. Robert explained. "Where do you go with Don?"

"We go in the door, turn left, go up the stairs and play in the big room at the end of the hall," Joey replied laying the picture of Patrick back onto the desk.

"What do you do with Don?" Dr. Robert asked.

"We have a big room to play in when I play with Don, so we usually throw a ball or play basketball," Joey said.

"Who wins when you play basketball?" Dr. Robert asked.

"It's hard to know sometimes because there isn't a basket. We have to hit a spot on the wall and call that a basket," Joey said.

"That's neat, playing basketball without a hoop," Dr. Robert said.

"Yeah, it's fun," Joey replied.

"What does Don look like?" Dr. Robert asked.

"He's about fifteen and real skinny. His teeth are all black and he said he has a problem with drugs and alcohol, but he has not used any of that stuff since he has been put in the building," Joey described.

"Did he tell you when he was put in the building, or how long he has been there?" Dr. Robert asked.

"No, I never asked," Joey replied.

"He hasn't done any bad stuff when I was there, though," Joey defended Don.

Dr. Robert pulled the drawing labeled "Don" and put it on the desk in front of Joey, "Do you recognize this room?"

"Yeah, that is the room that me and Don play in. Look at the spot on the wall. That's our basket," Joey said pointing at the drawing.

"Yeah, that's awesome," Dr. Robert replied.

Joey sat staring at the drawing for several minutes without saying a word.

"Joey, it appears as though our time is up for today. Would you be willing to come back and talk to me tomorrow?" Dr. Robert asked.

"Yeah, if it's OK with my mom," Joey said.

"Let's go find out," Dr. Robert said as he stood up and moved toward the door. Joey stood, followed Dr. Robert out the door and walked behind him to the waiting room where his mother was waiting.

"Hey big guy, how was it?" Sue asked Joey as he walked into the room.

"It was OK," Joey replied with a shrug of his shoulders.

"I was wondering if Joey could come back tomorrow and we could talk again?" Dr. Robert asked.

"I don't know, I haven't even got this approved with my insurance so I don't know how much they will cover," Sue explained.

"Oh, that's not a problem. I'll waive the fees for Joey, I just want him to be better," Dr. Robert told Sue hoping she would realize how intrigued he was by Joey's case.

"Well, I guess if Joey doesn't mind coming then I will bring him back," Sue replied looking down at Joey.

"I don't mind," Joey said looking up at his mom.

"I guess we'll see you tomorrow then," Sue said with a slight smile on her face.

"Great! Have a nice evening," Dr. Robert said in an excited tone.

Sue and Joey left the doctor's office and began their drive home.

"Is Dr. Robert nice to you?" Sue asked Joey.

"Yeah, he's OK," Joey responded.

"What do you talk about with him?" Sue inquired trying to find out more information.

"Mostly my dreams," Joey said.

"Does it bother you to talk to him?" Sue asked.

"No, he just asks me what happens and I tell him," Joey said blankly.

"Do you get upset talking about it?" Sue asked.

"No, he just lets me talk about it and shows me drawings of the building," Joey answered.

"Drawings? Drawings that he drew?" Sue asked.

"I don't think so, just pictures that someone drew," Joey said.

"You know you don't have to go back if you don't want to?" Sue asked.

"It's OK mom, he's nice," Joey reassured her.

Chapter Four

Talking about more Dreams

The next day after school, Sue was waiting for Joey in the parking lot. Joey came out of the building and looked around for his mother, finally seeing her sitting in her car waving at him.

"Hey mom," Joey said when he got in the car.

"Hey Joey, how was your day?" Sue asked.

"Fine," Joey answered.

"Are you ready to go see Dr. Robert?" Sue asked.

"Sure," Joey replied.

"Do you still want to go?" Sue asked.

"Sure," Joey repeated.

Sue drove Joey to Dr. Robert's office and walked him into the waiting room. She walked to the counter and said, "I have Joey here for his appointment."

"OK," the receptionist said as she pulled his file out of a drawer.

"Just have a seat, and I'll tell Dr. Robert you are here," the receptionist said as she walked out of the room.

"Hello," Dr. Robert said as he walked into the waiting room.

"Hi," Sue replied.

"Joey, are you ready to come talk to me for a little bit?" Dr. Robert asked.

"Sure," Joey replied.

"Dr. Robert, I have to run to the store. Will I have time while you are with Joey?" Sue asked.

"Yes, we will be here a little while. Do you have a cell phone?" Dr. Robert asked.

"Yeah," Sue answered.

"Just leave your cell phone number with me, and I'll call when we're close to being done," Dr. Robert said. Dr. Robert handed Sue a small piece of paper and she wrote her cell phone number on it.

"Great, I will call when we are getting close," Dr. Robert said.

Dr. Robert and Joey walk back to the office, and Dr. Robert sat behind his desk and Joey sat in the same seat as last time.

"Do you remember what we talked about yesterday?" Dr. Robert asked.

"Yes," Joey replied.

"Let's talk about someone different today. Tell me another person that you see in the building," Dr. Robert said.

"I meet with Eli sometimes, too," Joey said.

"Eli, what does he look like?" Dr. Robert asked.

"He's really old and sits in a wheelchair," Joey said.

"How old is 'really old?' Is he older than me?" Dr. Robert asked.

"Yeah, he's like eighty or ninety years old and always sits in a wheelchair," Joey explained.

"Is he paralyzed?" Dr. Robert asked.

"No, he's just old," Joey replied.

"If he's really old, then what do you and him do together?" Dr. Robert asked.

"He mostly just tells me stories," Joey replied.

"What kind of stories?" Dr. Robert asked.

"Mostly stories about being afraid, because he had to be in war," Joey said.

"War? What war was he in?" Dr. Robert asked.

"He said it was the first war and it was bad because he knew some of the people he was fighting," Joey responded.

"That must have been the Civil War. Did he say who he was fighting?" Dr. Robert asked.

"No, he just said he knew the people he fought and that he fought Indians too," Joey explained.

"Wow, a real Civil War soldier! What kind of things does he talk about?" Dr. Robert inquired further.

"He talked about working on the farm, meeting his wife, but mostly how scared he was when he had to shoot at people. He always said he wished he could forget that stuff," Joey said.

"Is that all you do with him, talk?" Dr. Robert asked.

"Yeah, he can't do anything else," Joey replied.

"Where do you and he talk?" Dr. Robert asked.

"He takes me toward the end of the building, and he stares out the window at the end of the hall," Joey said.

"You don't go into any rooms or anything?" Dr. Robert asked.

"No, just in the hallway," Joey replied.

"Look at this drawing Joey, is this the place you sit and talk?" Dr. Robert asked.

"Yeah, that's exactly it," Joey anxiously replied. "How did you get all these drawings of the places I go?" Joey asked.

"I'll tell you when we are done talking about your dreams, OK?" Dr. Robert said.

"OK," Joey said in a disappointed tone.

"So tell me who else you see at the building?" Dr. Robert asked.

"No one else," Joey replied.

"There is no one else that you talk to at the asylum?" Dr. Robert asked, accidently mentioning that the building Joey had been dreaming about was an asylum.

"Asylum! What's an asylum?" Joey asked in almost a yelling tone.

"It's called the Trans-Allegheny Lunatic Asylum and it was an old mental hospital," Dr. Robert explained.

"You mean it was a place for crazy people?" Joey asked.

"Well, it was a place for people with mental disorders," Dr. Robert said.

"Doesn't that mean they are crazy?" Joey insisted

"No, it just means they need help," Dr. Robert said.

"Why am I dreaming about that place?" Joey asked.

"I don't know I am trying to figure that out," Dr. Robert said.

"Are the people I see in my dreams crazy?" Joey asked.

"I don't know who they are, I will try to find out for you though," Dr Robert reassured Joey. "Let's get back to your dreams."

"OK," Joey replied.

"Who else do you talk to?" Dr. Robert asked.

Joey hesitated for a minute, looked down and said, "No one."

"So there are only three people who meet you at the door?" Dr. Robert asked.

"Yeah," Joey said in an uncertain tone.

"What if I told you that I thought there was one more person?" Dr. Robert said.

"I don't know," Joey replied.

"You don't know what?" Dr. Robert asked.

"Don't make me talk about her - she's evil," Joey said in an almost sad tone.

"What's her name?" Dr. Robert asked.

"Her name is Sharon," Joey said as he shivered.

"Why is she evil?" Dr. Robert asked.

"I don't know why, she is just evil," Joey replied.

"What does she do that makes her evil?" Dr. Robert asked.

"She wants to take me into an evil place," Joey said.

"Where is the evil place?" Dr. Robert continued.

"The tunnel!" Joey replied.

"What is so evil about the tunnel?" Dr. Robert asked.

"When I first went with Sharon, she took me down into the basement and through the doors to the tunnel. Everything was fine until we got inside the tunnel, and in the dark, there were ghosts or spirits or something," Joey explained.

"Where is the tunnel?" Dr. Robert asked.

"It is in the basement of the building," Joey replied.

Dr. Robert pulled out the fifth and final drawing and laid it on the desk in front of Joey.

"No!" Joey yelled as he looked away.

"Joey, are you OK?" Dr. Robert asked.

"That's it! Where did that drawing come from?" Joey asked.

"To be honest Joey, all of these drawings were done by you," Dr. Robert explained.

"Not me, I can't draw," Joey said.

"The first day we met I found these pictures on my desk," Dr. Robert told Joey.

"I didn't draw them!" Joey insisted.

"OK, can you tell me more about Sharon?" Dr. Robert asked.

"No," Joey replied.

"No you don't know, or no you don't want to talk about it?" Dr. Robert asked.

"I don't want to talk about it," Joey said.

"I will make you a deal. You give me a physical description of Sharon, and we'll call your mom so you can leave," Dr. Robert offered.

"I just have to describe her and then I can leave?" Joey confirmed.

"Yes, just tell me what she looks like and you can leave," Dr. Robert agreed.

"She is about this much shorter than you," Joey said, holding up his thumb and index fingers to indicate almost four inches. "She has bright red hair, and she looks about fifty years old."

"Is she mean to you?" Dr. Robert asked.

"No, she just wants me to go down in the tunnel," Joey replied.

"What do the ghosts look like?" Dr. Robert asked.

"You said I didn't have to talk about that!" Joey insisted.

"You're right, I'm sorry. What color eyes does Sharon have?" Dr. Robert tried staying on task with his questions.

"They are black until she gets to the tunnel and then they turn bright red like they are on fire," Joey described.

"What does she wear?" Dr. Robert asked.

"A long black dress," Joey replied.

Dr. Robert finished documenting what Joey had said and realized Joey was too uncomfortable talking about Sharon so he decided to change the subject. "School's almost over, are you excited for summer break?"

"Yeah, I don't have anything planned except going to the pool," Joey said.

"Are you ready to go see if your mom's here?" Dr. Robert asked.

"Sure," Joey replied.

Dr. Robert walked over and opened the door, waiting for Joey to walk through. Joey walked out and opened the door to the waiting room.

"Hey mom," Joey said walking into the waiting room.

"Hey honey, are you ready to go?" Sue asked.

"You made it back, did you?" Dr. Robert asked.

"It didn't take me as long as I thought," Sue replied.

"Can I talk to you alone for a just a second before you go?" Dr. Robert asked.

"Sure. Joey, sit down there for a minute and let me talk to Dr. Robert," Sue said.

Dr. Robert opened the door for Sue as they step into the back hallway.

"I wanted to tell you that Joey started talking about some things that were scaring him in his dreams, so you may keep an eye on him tonight," Dr. Robert said.

"Is he OK?" Sue asked.

"Yes, I am just working on figuring out what is bothering him and then I will work on helping him deal with it," Dr. Robert said, trying not to alarm Sue.

"OK, I'll let you know what happens," Sue said.

"I don't think he needs to come back for a week or so, he needs to take a break," Dr. Robert said.

"OK, I will call the first of next week and make an appointment," Sue said.

"That will be fine," Dr. Robert replied.

Chapter Five

Joey's Dreams Continue

Later that evening, Joey was in his bedroom doing his homework when his mom walked in "Hey buddy, are you busy?"

"Just finishing my homework," Joey replied.

"Can I talk to you for a minute?" Sue asked sitting down on the side of Joey's bed.

"Sure mom," Joey said as he shut his book and turned around to face her.

"Dr. Robert told me that he was helping you work on your bad dream problem. Is he really helping you?" Sue asked.

"I don't know mom, we just talk. I just sit and talk about my dreams," Joey said.

"Does he talk about things you don't want to talk about?" Sue asked.

"No, just about my dreams," Joey said.

"OK, if anything happens that makes you feel uncomfortable let me know," Sue said.

"OK mom," Joey replied.

Sue got up and walked out of the room, still very concerned about Joey. Joey put his pajamas on and climbed into bed.

"No, I don't want to go! Get away from me!" Joey's voice echoed through the night air.

"Joey, are you OK?" Sue screamed as she rushed through the dark house. Sue burst through the bedroom door to see Joey tossing around in a pool of sweat. She sat on the edge of the bed and grabbed his arms.

"Joey!" Sue yelled at Joey trying to wake him up.

Joey stops yelling and goes limp in bed, "Mom?" Joey asked.

"Are you OK?" Sue asked.

"Yeah, I just had a bad dream," Joey said.

"Was it the same dream?" Sue asked.

"Yeah, it was the scary one," Joey replied.

"Do you want me to call Dr. Robert and see if he can see you tomorrow?" Sue asked.

"No, it was just one dream. Maybe if I have more we can call him later," Joey said.

"Are you going to be able to sleep tonight?" Sue asked.

"Yeah, the dream only lasts until I wake up," Joey said smiling.

"OK smarty pants, I love you," Sue said as she kissed Joey on the forehead.

"Night mom, love you too," Joey said.

Dr. Robert sat in his office studying the drawings and tried to figure out if there may be some hidden meaning in them. He stared at the picture labeled "Sharon", trying to figure out why all the pictures were in exact detail except "Sharon". He recalled the door facing to the exact detail, the doors to exact detail - but it was not a tunnel but a room. Dr. Robert decided that the only way he could solve the problem was to take Joey to the asylum, so he decided to call Sue to get her approval.

"Hello," Sue answered the phone.

"Sue? This is Dr. Robert," he said.

"Hi Dr. Robert, is everything OK?" She asked.

"Yeah, everything is fine. I wanted to ask you a question," Dr. Robert said.

"What's that?" Sue asked.

"I was wondering if you would let Joey go visit the Trans-Allegheny Lunatic Asylum with me?" Dr. Robert asked.

"I don't know. I'm not sure I want him to go there. My son is still having bad dreams about that place." Sue said.

"I think it would be a therapeutic trip for him. He can finally face some of the fears he has," Dr. Robert said.

"I'll talk to him when he comes home from school this afternoon and give you a call tomorrow," Sue said.

"That'll be fine. Let me know and I will arrange a tour for Saturday so he doesn't have to miss school," Dr. Robert said.

"OK, bye," Sue said.

"Goodbye," Dr. Robert said, hanging the phone up.

Chapter Six

Joey asked to go to the Asylum

Sue sat in her car waiting for Joey to come out of school and tossed the idea of him going to the asylum with Dr. Robert. She feared that Joey going to the asylum may have some negative effects on him. Sue decided that even though Joey was young, the decision would be his. Sue begins waving out the window as she sees Joey running down the side walk towards the car.

"Hey buddy, how was school?" Sue asked as Joey sat in the front seat beside her.

"Fine," Joey replied.

"Did you learn anything today?" Sue asked while she was pulling away from the school.

"No," Joey said. "Am I going back to Dr. Robert?"

"Not today. Do you want to go back to Dr. Robert?" Sue asked.

"I don't care," Joey replied.

"I'm glad you asked about Dr. Robert because he called today," Sue said.

"What did he want?" Joey asked.

"He wanted to know if you wanted to go visit the Trans-Allegheny Lunatic Asylum with him," Sue said.

"What did you tell him?" Joey asked.

"I told him that I would have to let you decide," Sue answered.

"Oh," Joey said.

"You don't have to go if you don't want to," Sue insisted.

"I don't know," Joey said.

"It's OK, baby. I don't want to rush you into a decision," Sue said.

"I'm hungry," Joey changed the subject.

"I have dinner ready at home," Sue said.

Sue and Joey arrived at their house, and Joey jumped out of the car and ran inside.

"Dad, I'm home," Joey yelled as he ran in the door.

"Hey pal, how was school today?" Jim asked.

"It was OK. I don't think I learned nothing though," Joey replied.

"Didn't learn nothing, is that right?" Jim joked with Joey.

"What's for dinner?" Joey asked.

"Hotdogs," Jim replied.

"Hotdogs are my favorite," Joey said.

"Wash your hands and head for the table," Sue told Joey.

Joey washed his hands and sat down at the table. Jim and Sue gathered the food, carried it to the table and sat down for dinner.

"What do you want on your hotdog?" Sue asked Joey.

"Ketchup," Joey replied.

"One hotdog with ketchup coming right up," Sue said.

"Thanks Mom," Joey said, taking the hotdog out of her hand.

They sat quietly at the table as they began eating their food.

"Did my Mom talk to you about what Dr. Robert wanted?" Jim asked.

"Yeah," Joey replied.

"What do you think?" Jim asked.

"He wants to think about it," Sue replied for Joey.

"It's OK if you want to think about it, we just want what you want," Jim explained.

"I'm just scared," Joey said.

"What are you afraid of?" Jim asked.

"Jim, leave it alone," Sue insisted.

"I'm just talking to him. I'm not forcing him to do anything," Jim replied looking at Sue.

"It's OK Mom. I don't mind talking about it," Joey said in a reassured tone.

"What is it that scares you about going to that place?" Jim asked.

"I don't have a problem with going to the asylum. It's just that there's a place there that scares me," Joey explained.

"What place is that?" Jim asked.

"It's in the basement," Joey said.

"What's so scary about it?" Jim asked.

"Jim, that's enough. Eat your dinner honey, we'll talk about this later," Sue interrupted.

"I don't care Mom. I was just telling dad how scared I get," Joey said.

"OK honey," Sue said.

"There is a tunnel in the basement, and it scares me," Joey explained.

"Well, if you want to go, just tell Dr. Robert you don't want to go into the basement," Jim said.

"I might," Joey said as he finished eating his hotdog.

"I'll call Dr. Robert tomorrow and explain what you want," Sue said.

"OK," Joey said.

The family finished eating their dinner, cleaned up the kitchen and settled in for a relaxing evening watching TV.

"OK guys, we have to get up early in the morning, so it's time for bed," Sue said as she stood up and waited for Jim and Joey to stand up.

"Night big guy," Jim said.

"Night Dad," Joey said as he jumped up on his lap and kissed him on the cheek. Joey ran to his bedroom with Sue following close behind.

Joey got ready for bed while Sue folded some of his clothes and put them in his dresser. He ran out of the bathroom and jumped into his bed and pulled the covers over him.

"Good night, little man," Sue said as she kissed him on the forehead.

"Night Mom, love you," Joey replied.

"Love you too, sweet dreams," Sue said as she walked out the door and turned off the light.

Sue walked back into the living room and sat back down beside Jim.

"What do you think about him going to that asylum with Dr. Robert?" Sue asked.

"I don't know. If there is a chance of him getting rid of the nightmares, I want him to go," Jim said.

"I agree, but what if it gets worse?" Sue asked.

"How can it get worse? He dreams almost every night and he is having two or three nightmares a week now," Jim said.

"OK, I will call Dr. Robert in the morning and have him arrange it for a Saturday so Joey won't have to miss school," Sue agreed.

"Are you ready for bed?" Jim said, yawning.

"I'm waiting on you," Sue said, laughing as they both go to bed.

"I don't want to go! You can't make me! Let go!" Joey screamed into the darkness.

"What's wrong Joey?" Sue yelled, running into Joey's bedroom and turning on the light.

"I'm OK! I'm OK!" Joey replied, realizing that he had a nightmare but was home safe.

"What is it?" Sue demanded.

"What is what?" Joey said in a confused tone.

"What are you dreaming about? What is scaring you so bad?" Sue asked.

"It's the asylum. She wants me to go into the tunnel," Joey said.

"Why do you keep having this nightmare," Sue said in an exhausted tone.

"It's OK Mommy, Dr. Robert will help me get rid of them," Joey said.

"It's OK baby, just go back to sleep," Sue said as she stood up and walked back to bed.

"Is he OK?" Jim asked Sue as she crawled back into bed.

"Another bad dream. I hope Dr. Robert can help him," Sue replied.

The following morning Sue wasted no time calling Dr. Robert.

"Dr. Robert's office," A female's voice answered the phone.

"Can I talk to Dr. Robert please?" Sue asked.

"Sure, may I tell him who's calling?" the female voice asked.

"Tell him I'm calling on behalf of Joey," Sue said.

"OK, please hold," the female voice said as she put Sue on hold.

"Dr. Robert speaking," Dr. Robert answered the phone.

"Dr. Robert, this is Sue, Joey's mom," Sue said.

"How is Joey?" Dr. Robert asked.

"Joey is fine but he is still having the nightmares," Sue explained.

"How often is he having the bad ones?" Dr. Robert said.

"Three or four times a week now. We talked about your idea of taking him to the asylum and we thought that might be a good idea," Sue said.

"I think if we have him face some of his fears, the nightmares will go away," Dr. Robert said.

"I hope so," Sue replied.

"Great, how about if I pick him up around eight on Saturday?" Dr. Robert asked.

"That would be fine. I will have him ready," Sue said.

"I will do all I can to help him," Dr. Robert reassured Sue.

"I appreciate your help Dr. Robert, I will see you on Saturday," Sue said.

"OK, I'll see you on Saturday," Dr. Robert said and then hung up the phone.

Chapter Seven

Dr. Robert confirms tour of Asylum

Dr. Robert pulled his notes out of Joey's file and looked up the number for the Trans-Allegheny Lunatic Asylum.

"Trans-Allegheny Lunatic Asylum, this is Rebecca. How may I help you?" Rebecca said.

"Rebecca, this is Dr. Robert. I was wondering if you could give me and a young boy a tour of the asylum on Saturday morning around nine?" Dr. Robert asked.

"I could arrange for you to have a tour," Rebecca said.

"I really need someone who knows everything about the asylum," Dr. Robert insisted.

"I don't mind helping you how I can, but you need to tell me a little more about what is going on," Rebecca said.

"I am bound by patient confidentiality, but I will tell you that the young boy I am bringing has never been to the asylum and has first hand details about the inside of the building," Dr. Robert explained.

"Is it about the ghosts?" Rebecca asked.

"Ghosts? What are you talking about?" Dr. Robert asked.

"Are you familiar with the Trans-Allegheny Lunatic Asylum?" Rebecca asked.

"Just what I read on the Internet," Dr. Robert said.

"This building houses some of the most outrageous claims that I have ever heard. I have heard stories as simple as voices in the halls and as extreme as people getting dragged down the hall," Rebecca said.

"What are you trying to say? The asylum is haunted?" Dr. Robert asked.

"I have no first-hand knowledge but I have been told stories about the asylum," Rebecca said.

"Would you tell me some of those stories?" Dr. Robert asked.

"I suppose the most common report to us is seeing a dark shadow moving around different areas of the asylum. It is not always in the same area, and it does not form a shape, it is like a black cloud," Rebecca said.

"Do you think that it's just their eyes playing tricks on them?" Dr. Robert asked.

"No, I know I said I haven't seen anything. But I will admit to you that I have seen the black cloud, and it is real," Rebecca said.

"Wow, what else has happened?" Dr. Robert asked.

"We give tours here at the asylum, and one day when one of the guides was walking through the hall, she pointed to one of the rooms that used to be used for exams. When she pointed she said it felt like someone grabbed her arm and dragged her into the room. There were twelve people on the tour that verified that she was moved by some other force than her own," Rebecca said.

"What happened when she was pulled into the room?" Dr. Robert asked.

"Nothing, she was pulled into one of the old examination rooms and just released," Rebecca said.

"That's amazing. Have you ever had anyone check out the asylum to see if it was haunted?" Dr. Robert asked.

"Yes, as a matter of fact I did. I invited a television ghost hunting team to the asylum and they were pretty positive that the asylum has some sort of spirits wondering the halls. They didn't say if they were good or bad, but they said they were definitely present," Rebecca said.

"Did they get any solid evidence?" Dr. Robert asked.

"I don't think they got any good video, but I know they got a good bit of audio recordings," Rebecca said.

"I don't believe in that kind of stuff," Dr. Robert said.

"I didn't either until we bought the asylum," Rebecca replied.

"Is there anything else I should know about the asylum?" Dr. Robert asked.

"The asylum has housed thousands of patients, and in the early years, there was talk about the doctors doing some experimental surgeries on some of the patients," Rebecca said.

"What do you mean experimental surgeries?" Dr. Robert asked.

"As you can imagine back in the late 1800's and early 1900's, most people put mentally ill, mentally retarded, drug addicts, and alcoholic people in the asylum. It was a catch-all for people with things wrong with them, legitimate or not, and they would put them in the asylum and never look back. The common rule, from what I understand, was two years without contact from a relative made them fair game for the surgeons. The surgeons performed hundreds of lobotomies and unnecessary brain surgeries on the patients," Rebecca explained.

"Wasn't anyone responsible for overseeing the surgeons?" Dr. Robert asked.

"No, this was a state facility. Back in those days they didn't care," Rebecca said.

"Did all the patients die?" Dr. Robert asked.

"No, actually most of them lived and died of natural causes," Rebecca said.

"What happened to the patients when they died?" Dr. Robert asked.

"Up until the early 1970's no one knows what happened to the patients who died in the asylum," Rebecca replied.

"How did they get away with not keeping track of the people that died?" Dr. Robert asked.

"I don't know. You would think people would miss them and complain," Rebecca replied.

"Do you think these dead people missing from the property are the spirits haunting the asylum," Dr. Robert asked.

"I thought you didn't believe in that kind of stuff," Rebecca asked.

"I am trying to keep an open mind," Dr. Robert explained.

"I think the spirits are from patients who died here," Rebecca said.

"There are no official records for the early years, and it wasn't until the mid 1950's before the state had to record all patients entering and leaving the asylum," Rebecca said.

"I am glad you told me this information. I will keep an open eye on Saturday," Dr. Robert said.

"OK, I will meet you at the front entrance at nine," Rebecca said.

Chapter Eight

Going to the Asylum

On Saturday morning Dr. Robert pulled in front of Joey's house and walked to the front door. As he started to knock on the door it flew open.

"Good morning Dr. Robert," Joey said.

"Good morning Joey. Are you ready for our field trip today?" Dr. Robert asked.

"Yea," Joey replied.

"Joey, run upstairs and get your jacket," Sue said, walking to the door behind Joey.

"OK Mom," Joey said as he ran upstairs.

"Take care of him, I don't want him traumatized," Sue said.

"I'll try not to let him get scared," Dr. Robert said.

"You better try hard," Sue insisted with a serious look on her face.

"I'm ready," Joey yelled, making his way to the door with his jacket.

"OK, have a good time buddy, and I will see you in a little bit," Sue said, kissing Joey's cheek.

"OK Mom, love you, bye," Joey spurted out as he started walking toward the car.

"You have my cell phone number if you need anything," Dr. Robert said.

"Be careful," Sue yelled as they loaded into the car and pulled away.

Settling in the car as they began their journey, Dr. Robert asked, "Do you want to listen to some music?"

"Sure," Joey said.

Dr. Robert turned on the radio and tuned it to a classic rock-n-roll station.

"How do you feel?" Dr. Robert asked.

"OK," Joey replied.

"Are you excited or afraid?" Dr. Robert asked.

"I'm both," Joey said.

"Me too," Dr. Robert said.

"Why are you afraid?" Joey asked.

"I don't know why I'm scared. I guess because I don't know what's going to happen." Dr. Robert replied.

"We'll be OK," Joey said.

Dr. Robert smiled at him. After several minutes of silence, Dr. Robert said, "We are getting close."

"OK," Joey replied.

Dr. Robert drove the car in front of the building where Joey could see the sign.

"Trans-Allegheny Lunatic Asylum," Joey read the sign out loud.

"What do you think?" Dr. Robert asked.

"It's big," Joey said.

"It sure is," Dr. Robert said.

"How do we get in?" Joey asked.

Dr. Robert smiled and they drove around to the front door, "Right in there."

"Oh," Joey said.

Dr. Robert parked his car, he and Joey got out and stretched their legs.

"This place is huge," Joey said.

"I know. It is bigger then any building I've ever seen," Dr. Robert replied.

Dr. Robert began walking toward the front entrance of the asylum with Joey following closely behind him.

"Good morning," A female voice came from behind them.

Dr. Robert and Joey quickly spin around.

"Good morning, Rebecca," Dr. Robert said as Rebecca walked closer to them.

"Rebecca, this is my friend Joey," Dr. Robert said.

"Hello, Joey, my name is Rebecca," Rebecca said holding out her hand.

"Hello Rebecca," Joey replied, shaking Rebecca's hand.

"If you gentlemen will follow me we will begin the tour," Rebecca said.

"Rebecca, if you don't mind I would like to do something a little unorthodox today and let Joey lead the tour," Dr. Robert requested.

"That's fine with me. Are you up to it Joey?" Rebecca asked.

"No, I don't know anything about this place," Joey said.

"Joey, I think if you walk inside the door you will have someone there to help you," Dr. Robert said.

Joey stood in front of the building, looking up in awe at the incredible size of the building.

"It's just like I remember," Joey said.

"I thought you said he has never been here?" Rebecca asked.

"He hasn't. But he did dream about it," Dr. Robert replied.

"Joey, how do you feel?" Dr. Robert asked.

"Relieved," Joey replied.

"What do you mean relieved?" Dr. Robert asked.

"I have dreamed about this place so long that I am glad to finally see it," Joey said.

"Are you ready to go inside?" Dr. Robert asked.

"I think I am," Joey responded.

"The doors are unlocked so we can go in," Rebecca said.

Dr. Robert walked in front of Joey and Rebecca as they walked to the front door of the asylum. Dr. Robert opened the door and stepped into the foyer, "Come on in."

Joey stepped into the asylum, with Rebecca close behind him. Joey stopped and stared towards the back of the foyer.

"What is it?" Dr. Robert asked.

"It's Patrick," Joey said in a scared tone.

"Where is he?" Dr. Robert asked as Rebecca moved behind him.

"He's right there in front of us, don't you see him?" Joey said pointing straight ahead of him.

"No Joey, we can't see him," Dr. Robert said.

"No Patrick, I am talking to Dr. Robert," Joey said looking forward. "He is standing right in front of you," Joey insisted.

"Joey, I can't see him," Dr. Robert said again.

"I was talking to Patrick, he can't see you either," Joey said.

"Is he talking to you?" Dr. Robert asked.

"Yes, can't you hear him?" Joey asked.

"No, I can't hear him," Dr. Robert said.

"Why can't we see him?" Rebecca asked.

"I don't know," Dr. Robert answered.

"Joey, what normally happens in your dream?" Dr. Robert asked.

"We just walk down to the room where we play," Joey replied.

"OK, go ahead and walk down to the room with him," Dr. Robert said.

"OK," Joey said.

"Ask him where he is from," Dr. Robert said.

"Patrick, where do you live?" Joey asked. "He lives here."

"Ask him if he has always lived here," Dr. Robert said as they continued to walk down the corridor.

"Have you always lived here?" Joey asked as if he was talking into the air.

"Patrick said that as long as he can remember, he has lived here," Joey replied.

Reaching the end of the hall, Joey entered into the room and immediately stopped.

"What's wrong?" Dr. Robert, who was standing behind Joey, asked.

"It's different, everything is old," Joey said. "There usually is doctor stuff lying around and everything is shiny and new. Everything in here now is old," Joey said.

"Can you still see Patrick?" Rebecca asked.

"No, he disappeared when he entered the room," Joey said.

"So there is no one in the room?" Dr. Robert asked.

"No, just us," Joey said.

"What do we do now?" Rebecca asked.

"I think we need to go back to the main entrance," Dr. Robert said.

Rebecca began walking back toward the entrance of the asylum with Dr. Robert and Joey close behind.

Chapter Nine

Visiting the Dreams

Rebecca arrives at the front entrance first and turns and looks at Dr. Robert.

"Go on outside," Dr. Robert said.

Rebecca turns and heads out of the front door as Dr. Robert and Joey follow close behind.

"Why was that like that?" Joey asked.

"I don't know for sure but I have a theory about it. I think that in your dreams you actually go into the spirit world and when we showed up here Patrick had to manifest into the physical world," Dr. Robert explained.

"That makes sense," Rebecca said.

"I think I know what you mean," Joey said.

"My second theory will be confirmed when we walk back through the door," Dr. Robert said.

"What theory?" Rebecca asked.

"My theory is, when we walk back through the door, there will be another person waiting," Dr. Robert said.

"What if there is no one there?" Rebecca asked.

"Let's walk in and find out," Dr. Robert said confidently as he walked back toward the door.

"Wait," Rebecca said.

Dr. Robert turned and looked back at Rebecca with Joey standing beside him.

"What if there is something there and it's evil? Obviously these spirits use Joey as a portal to the physical world, what stops the evil ones from coming through?" Rebecca asked.

"I am betting on the fact that there have only been four spirits that have contacted Joey and that is all he will see," Dr. Robert said.

"OK, but if you are wrong this tour ends!" Rebecca said.

Dr. Robert opens the door and steps back into the foyer area. He surveys the room and then says "It's clear come, back in."

Joey and Rebecca step back into the foyer area.

"Hey," Joey said looking at a different area of the foyer.

"What do you see," Dr. Robert asked.

"I see Eli sitting right over there in his wheelchair," Joey said, pointing towards the back of the foyer.

"Is he saying anything?" Dr. Robert asked.

"He is waiting for me to push him down to our spot," Joey said.

"Go ahead and push him to where he wants to go," Dr. Robert said.

Joey walks over to the far side of the foyer and extends his arms in front of him, and it appears as if he is actually pushing a wheelchair. Dr. Robert watched closely at his posture and then noticed that Joey's hands appeared to be clinched around invisible handles. Joey continues to the southern end of the hallway and then stops. Joey walked as if the wheelchair were sitting in front of him, circling around and sat down on the window ledge.

"What is he doing?" Dr. Robert asked.

"He's looking out the window. He likes to look out the window for a few minutes, then he thinks of a story to tell me," Joey said as he looked out the window.

Dr. Robert and Rebecca stood a few feet away from Joey and stared at the location the wheel chair would be in, trying to imagine what Joey was looking at.

"Ask him if he sees us," Dr. Robert said.

"Eli, I have friends with me today. Can you see them?" Joey asked.

Joey sat quiet for a minute and said, "No, he can't see you."

"Ask him if you can tell us one of his stories," Dr. Robert said.

"Can I repeat the story to my friends?" Joey asked. Joey then sat quiet for a minute before beginning to tell the story that Eli was telling.

"It was in the winter, the first year of the war, when I was sent to deliver a message to a small place called Jane Lew, Virginia. It was so cold that if you opened your mouth, your spit froze. I remember getting on my horse and feeling how cold the leather was on my hind quarters. I lived about twenty miles from Jane Lew so I knew if I left early I could get back late that night, or I could stay in Jane Lew. I rode pretty hard the first couple hours but then I saw enemy troops coming up the road, so I headed up into the woods. They must have been too cold to shoot straight because they shot at me, but didn't hit me. It scared me so much that I made my horse run the rest of the way to Jane Lew. When I got to Jane Lew, I went to the headquarters, and I handed the captain the note, and he sat down and read it. The captain blankly looked out the window for a few seconds and then looked at me. 'You're excused,' the captain said. I turned to walk out and heard him tearing the paper into pieces. I don't know what the letter said, but it made me mad that I risked my life for him to tear the letter up." Joey repeated Eli.

"What is he doing now?" Dr. Robert asked.

"He is just staring off out the window," Joey said.

"What happens now?" Dr Robert asked.

"We just sit and look out the window," Joey said, turning his head back toward the window.

Dr. Robert and Rebecca stood and watched Joey for a couple of minutes and then began looking out the window, trying to figure out what he was looking at.

"He's gone," Joey said, as he looked back toward where he parked the wheelchair.

"Where is he?" Rebecca asked.

"I don't know. He just wasn't there when I turned back around," Joey said.

"OK, let's take a break for lunch. Are you hungry Joey?" Dr. Robert said.

"Yeah," Joey replied.

"Rebecca, is there any place to eat around here?" Dr. Robert said.

"What do you want? We have fast food, sit-down restaurants, and we even have a hot dog place right down the road," Rebecca told them.

"What do you want Joey?" Dr. Robert asked.

"I like hotdogs," Joey replied.

"Hotdogs it is. Rebecca if you would like to go with us, it would be my pleasure to buy you lunch," Dr. Robert offered.

"I would like that," Rebecca answered.

Dr. Robert, Joey and Rebecca got into the car and they drove down to the exit of the asylum. Dr. Robert stopped at the main road and asked Rebecca, "Which way?"

"Turn left and then it's about a half a mile up on the left," Rebecca said.

Dr. Robert pulled onto the road and drove toward the restaurant without conversation. Pulling into the parking lot Dr. Robert said, "'Joe's Hotdog House,' Joey I didn't know you had a hotdog house."

"I don't," Joey said in a serious tone.

"I'm just kidding because of the name of the restaurant," Dr. Robert said.

"Oh, I get it," Joey replied blankly.

Rebecca and Dr. Robert smiled, realizing the innocence of Joey.

"What do you want to eat?" Dr. Robert asked.

"A hotdog with ketchup," Joey replied.

"A hotdog with ketchup, and for you sir?" the cashier asked Dr. Robert.

"I'll have two hotdogs and make mine with only ketchup also," Dr. Robert said smiling at Joey.

"I would like one hotdog with only ketchup too," Rebecca said smiling.

"Three ice teas, please," Dr. Robert said.

The cashier took the money and handed Dr. Robert his change.

"Where do you want to sit Joey?" Dr. Robert asked.

"Here," Joey replied, climbing into a booth.

Rebecca slid into the booth across from Joey, and Dr. Robert sat down beside Rebecca.

"Hotdog with ketchup," Dr. Robert said, sliding a hotdog in front of Joey.

"Thank you," Joey quietly said.

"And a hotdog for you," Dr. Robert said, handing Rebecca a hotdog.

"Thank you Dr. Robert," Rebecca said.

"You are both welcome," Dr. Robert said.

They sat quietly eating their hotdogs, looking around at the old style hotdog house.

"What's your plan for this afternoon?" Rebecca asked, looking at Dr. Robert.

"I figured we could go and let Joey go back into the asylum to see if he sees anyone else," Dr. Robert said.

"What if he doesn't see anyone?" Rebecca asked.

"Then we're done. This experiment is unprecedented. I'm just taking this one step at a time," Dr. Robert said.

"How was your hotdog, Joey?" Rebecca asked.

"It was fine," Joey replied.

"Are you ready to go?" Dr. Robert asked.

"Yeah," Joey replied.

"Let's get out of here," Rebecca said in a joking tone.

Dr. Robert, Rebecca and Joey get up and start toward the door. Leaving the restaurant, Dr. Robert steps into the parking lot, stretches and then sits down in the car.

"Do you mind going back to the asylum, Joey?" Dr. Robert asked.

"No, that's OK," Joey answered.

"What about you, Rebecca? Do you have time to keep going with us?" Dr. Robert asked.

"The Trans-Allegheny Lunatic Asylum has become my life. I don't have anything else to do," Rebecca explained.

"Great, I guess our quest will continue," Dr. Robert said.

Dr. Robert drove back to the hospital and parked back in the same spot he previously had. Dr. Robert, Rebecca and Joey got out of the car and paused, looking at the front of the asylum.

"This is truly an immaculate building," Dr. Robert said.

"I think what makes it so interesting to me is the history behind it," Rebecca added.

"If the walls of this building could talk, I bet they would tell some crazy stories," Dr. Robert said.

Rebecca walked to the front doors and turned to Dr. Robert and Joey and said, "Are you guys ready?"

"I think we are," Dr. Robert said, looking at Joey.

"Yeah," Joey replied.

Dr. Robert let Joey walk to the door first and then followed closely behind him into the foyer of the asylum.

"Do you see anything or anyone?" Dr. Robert asked.

"Yeah, Don is here," Joey said.

"Where is he?" Dr. Robert asked.

"He's right beside me waiting for me to follow him," Joey said as he began to walk down the hall.

"Ask him where he's from," Dr. Robert said walking behind Joey.

"Where did you live before you came here?" Joey asked as he started down the hallway.

After a minute of silence, Joey turned to Dr. Robert and said, "He lived in Parkersburg."

Joey entered the auditorium and walked to the front of the room. He sat down on the edge of the stage and asked, "What do we do now?"

"Why?" Dr. Robert asked.

"When I walked in the door, he disappeared. I don't know where he went," Joey said.

"Is this room like you remembered it?" Dr. Robert asked.

"Yeah, only it looked newer," Joey said.

"Where did you shoot basketball?" Dr. Robert asked.

Joey pointed to a worn place on the wall where the West Virginia state seal had been painted.

"That makes a good basket," Dr. Robert told him.

"Do you see anyone else?" Rebecca asked.

"No," Joey replied.

"Why don't we go back outside and figure out our next move," Dr. Robert said.

"OK," Joey said as he confidently walked out the door of the auditorium and headed down the hallway.

Dr. Robert and Rebecca walk several feet behind Joey, Rebecca leaned over to Dr. Robert and whispered "Is he going to be OK?"

"Yeah, but I just don't know what I can do to stop his nightmares," Dr. Robert said.

Joey continued to walk out the door with Dr. Robert and Rebecca following. As the three walked out into the sunshine, Joey slowly walked back toward the car.

"Hey Joey, where are you going?" Dr. Robert asked.

"Home," Joey replied.

"Why you going home?" Dr. Robert asked.

"I don't want to go back inside," Joey answered.

"Why?" Dr. Robert asked.

"Because," Joey evasively answered.

"Oh, I remember. The only one left is Sharon," Dr. Robert said.

"Sharon, who's that?" Rebecca asked.

"Sharon is the person that tries to take Joey down into the tunnel. The tunnel must hold some type of evil spirits because it terrorizes Joey to talk about it," Dr. Robert said.

"What are you going to do?" Rebecca asked.

"Joey, are you ready to go home?" Dr. Robert asked.

"Yeah," Joey answered.

"Why don't you hop in the car, and I'll be there in a second," Dr. Robert said.

Joey climbed in the car and closed the door.

"Is there any way you can pull up the records and try to find Don, Eli and Patrick?" Dr. Robert asked.

"Yeah, I'll pull my files and see if I can match any of the records. I'll look tonight and I'll give you a call tomorrow," Rebecca said.

"That will be fine," Dr. Robert said shaking Rebecca's hand and then walking to the car.

"Bye Joey," Rebecca yelled through the car glass at Joey. Joey waved at Rebecca.

Dr. Robert got into the car and started the engine.

"Long day, wasn't it?" Dr. Robert said, trying to make conversation with Joey.

"Yeah," Joey replied.

"What do you think about what happened today?" Dr. Robert asked.

"It was OK," Joey said.

"Do you feel any better about your dreams?" Dr. Robert asked.

"Yeah, I'm still scared about Sharon," Joey said.

"I don't know if being at the asylum will help get rid of your dreams but I hope it does," Dr. Robert explained.

"I hope so too," Joey replied.

Dr. Robert dropped Joey off without further discussion about the asylum.

Chapter Ten

Checking the Files

Dr. Robert got up early the next day and called Rebecca.

"Hello," Rebecca answered the phone.

"Rebecca, this is Dr. Robert. I know it's early, but I called to see if you had found any information on our asylum patients?" Dr. Robert asked.

"No, I have not even started looking yet. The files are in boxes, and I have to go through them one box at a time," Rebecca said.

"Would you like me to come over and help you?" Dr. Robert asked.

"Sure, you're welcome to come and help," Rebecca said.

"I can be there in about an hour," Dr. Robert said.

"I'll see you in a little bit. When you come to the asylum, drive around the right side of the building and park in the back. I will meet you there," Rebecca said and hung up the phone.

Dr. Robert gathered his files and headed for the asylum. While on his way to the asylum he kept running Joey's experiences through his mind. Trying to figure out what Joey could provide for the spirits to satisfy them, wondering why they are using Joey as a portal to the physical world. Dr. Robert pulled into the asylum parking lot, continued around the right side of the building and parked near the rear entrance.

"Hey," Rebecca yells, stepping out the back door.

"Hey," Dr. Robert said, back as he got out of the car.

"I see you made it," Rebecca said.

"Yeah, it was an easy drive," Dr. Robert said grabbing a file from the passenger seat.

"Come on in, I had all the files brought into the conference room," Rebecca said, holding the door open.

"Great," Dr. Robert said, walking in the door.

As Dr. Robert entered the conference room he noticed boxes of files stacked three deep against the walls of the room. They were packed in the boxes and labeled by the years the patients were in the asylum.

"Where do we start?" Dr. Robert asked, overwhelmed by the amount of files.

"I say we just start at the beginning and go from there," Rebecca said.

Rebecca grabs a box and sets it on the table, "Our first victim."

Dr. Robert pulls the lid of the box off and blows the dust off.

"Wow, there are some really old files in here," Dr. Robert observed.

Dr. Robert and Rebecca both grab a hand full of files and start leafing through the pages.

"Just remember that the asylum was not required to keep records, so there may not be files on every patient," Rebecca said.

They continued to look at files for a couple of hours before Rebecca said, "I think I got something."

"What is it?" Dr. Robert said.

"I found a file on Elijah J. Jackson from the late 1800's," Rebecca said.

"Why was he in the asylum?" Dr. Robert asked.

"He was diagnosed with insanity," Rebecca replied.

"What were his symptoms?" Dr. Robert said.

"It says that he came home from war and he was scared all the time. He later got so afraid he stopped sleeping and eating," Rebecca read.

"That has to be him," Dr. Robert said excitedly.

"It says he was committed in 1865 and lived there until he died in 1922," Rebecca continued from the file.

"Can I see the file?" Dr. Robert asked as he held out his hand.

"Sure," Rebecca said as she handed him the file.

Dr. Robert looked through the file and said, "This poor guy was here for fifty-seven years, and they didn't even take the time to write down a diagnosis. There is nothing about the guy in here except that no one came to see him, and he never received any treatment."

"Does it say what he died from?" Rebecca asked.

"No, but it looks as though he was old," Dr. Robert said.

"He sounds old," Rebecca replied.

"One down, three to go, I'll lay this file over there, and we'll continue looking for the other three," Dr. Robert said.

Dr. Robert tossed the file aside and they continued to search through the boxes. Dr. Robert and Rebecca would randomly find interesting files and read them out loud. They continued to search the files for a couple of hours.

"I need a break," Dr. Robert yawned.

"Me too," Rebecca replied.

"What do you say we go for a walk to wake up?" Dr. Robert asked.

"That should refresh us," Rebecca said as she moved toward the door.

Dr. Robert stepped out the door and looked around at the beautiful landscape that surrounded the asylum.

"What a beautiful location, how did you end up here?" Dr. Robert asked.

"I used to live in a small city in southern West Virginia when my dad came across the opportunity to buy this asylum. It was just one of those opportunities my dad could not pass up. I just came along to try to help him promote and make something of this old building. How did you end up here?" Rebecca asked.

"My story is pretty simple, my mom was a doctor and my dad was lawyer. I couldn't figure out what was wrong with me so I became a psychiatrist," Dr. Robert laughed.

"That's funny," Rebecca said.

"The truth is that I was raised in a pretty stable household with two parents. Weird for these times, isn't it?" Dr. Robert asked.

"I was too. We must be freaks by today's standards," Rebecca said.

"Yeah, are you ready to head back in?" Dr. Robert asked.

"Can't finish our work out here, can we?" Rebecca said.

They walked back to the rear entrance, and Dr. Robert opened the door and let Rebecca walk in the door in front of him.

"How far are we?" Dr. Robert asked.

"I think we are up to the mid 1920's" Rebecca replied.

Dr. Robert and Rebecca grabbed separate boxes of files and continued their search.

"Wow, the things they got away with back then, just incredible," Dr. Robert said, looking at an old file.

"What are you looking at?" Rebecca asked.

"This guy was brought to the hospital at the age of nineteen with a drinking problem. They did brain surgery on him and he ended up dying shortly after the operation. They listed the cause of death as 'natural'," Dr. Robert said.

"That's wild," Rebecca said looking back down at the files.

After searching the files for another thirty minutes Rebecca said, "I think I have something."

"What is it?" Dr. Robert said, looking up from which he was reading.

"A person named Patrick Harris was in his late 20's when he was brought to the asylum. He lived with his mom until she passed away and there was no one to take care of him. The neighbors brought him here," Rebecca explained.

"What was he diagnosed with?" Dr. Robert asked.

"He was mentally retarded," Rebecca read from a file.

"Does it say how he died?" Dr. Robert asked.

"It says that they did a routine operation and he died on the operating table," Rebecca read.

"They didn't have the equipment or technology that we have today," Dr. Robert said.

Rebecca laid Patrick' file down on top of "Elijah's" file and continued her search through the remaining files.

"I guess it's my lucky day, I found Donald Alvin and he was committed in 1989," Dr. Robert said.

"Why was he here?" Rebecca asked.

"He was addicted to drugs and alcohol. Listen to this! Donald died in the asylum in 1990 after he went through an experimental treatment program," Dr. Robert read.

"That makes three people, and all of them have died in the hospital," Rebecca said.

"I see the trend," Dr. Robert said.

"What if their deaths weren't an accident?" Rebecca asked.

"I don't know. It's looking suspicious, isn't it?" Dr. Robert asked. "We have one more person to find, Sharon."

"Sharon, the mystery woman," Rebecca joked.

"Wait a minute, how did you get all the way up to 1989?" Dr. Robert asked.

"I started randomly picking boxes," Rebecca said.

"I just finished this box. Which box is next?" Dr. Robert said, setting a box down beside Rebecca.

"Just grab one of the boxes on this side," Rebecca said, pointing toward the side wall.

Dr. Robert grabbed a random box and moved back to his chair. After several more minutes of searching, Dr. Robert said, "Jackpot."

"What did you find?" Rebecca asked as she stepped behind Dr. Robert to look over his shoulder.

"I found a file with the name 'Sharon' listed on it but the file is virtually empty. It says that she was admitted to asylum as an infant but was never diagnosed with a mental illness. It doesn't show any paperwork about who she was, where she was from, or what happened to her," Dr. Robert said.

"So we are no closer to finding Sharon than we were before," Rebecca said.

"I have no idea what we are going to do now," Dr. Robert said.

"I have an idea. According to the administrative records I looked at when I first moved here, there was always a hospital administrator in charge. In the late eighties and nineties, the state handled everything but before that, there was a man named Michael Miller. I have never met him, but some of the workers have told me that he still lives here in Weston," Rebecca said.

"Do you think he may know something about her?" Dr. Robert asked.

"According to the records, he started in the asylum back in the late twenties and retired in the eighties. I think it will be our best shot," Rebecca replied.

Dr. Robert and Rebecca straightened the boxes, then Dr. Robert followed Rebecca to her office.

"Grab a seat, I have his number somewhere," Rebecca said as she walked behind her desk and began leafing through her Rolodex.

"If he was the administrator for sixty some years, this guy must be old," Dr. Robert said.

"I don't know how old he is, but we will find out," Rebecca said, pulling a card out of her Rolodex.

Rebecca dialed the phone and waited for someone to answer the phone. "Hello," a female voice answered the phone.

"May I speak to Michael Miller?" Rebecca asked.

"OK... OK... I just had some questions about the old asylum," Rebecca said as she wrote on a piece of paper. "Thank you, that will be fine, have a nice day," Rebecca concluded and hung up the phone.

"What's going on?" Dr. Robert anxiously asked.

"I talked to a home health nurse who told me that Michael was now bedridden but he still has his mind. She said we could visit him if we wanted. He enjoys visitors," Rebecca said.

"Sounds good to me, do you know where he lives?" Dr. Robert asked.

"Yeah, he lives in a huge house at the south end of Main Street," Rebecca said.

"Is that far from here?" Dr. Robert asked.

"It's only about a mile," Rebecca said.

"I'll drive, you navigate," Dr. Robert said.

"Sounds good to me," Rebecca said as she walked out the door.

Dr. Robert and Rebecca got into his car and drove down through the middle of Weston and headed out to the south end of Main Street.

"It's the big green house coming up on your right," Rebecca said, pointing toward the house.

"I see it. That's a big house," Dr. Robert said.

"Yeah, I guess back in the day the asylum paid well," Rebecca said.

Dr. Robert parked in front of the two story wooden house with pillars running the height of the house. Dr. Robert and Rebecca exited the car and walked to the front door. Dr. Robert rang the door bell and waited for someone to answer.

"May I help you?" a young woman said, answering the door.

"I am Rebecca. I called from the asylum," Rebecca said.

"My name is Sandy, come in. I told him that you may come over, and he is anxious to talk to you," the woman said.

"Hi, I'm Dr. Robert," Dr. Robert said, holding out his hand.

"Welcome," Sandy said, shaking Dr. Robert's hand.

"Follow me. We moved his bedroom downstairs to keep from climbing the stairs all day," Sandy explained, leading them into the back of the house.

"How old is Mr. Miller," Dr. Robert asked.

"He will be ninety six in June," Sandy replied.

"Wow, that's impressive," Rebecca replied.

"Michael, are you awake?" Sandy said, walking into a large room that had been converted into a bedroom.

"I'm awake," Michael replied in a weak scruffy voice.

"You have some visitors," Sandy said.

"Is it that woman from the asylum?" Michael asked.

"Hello Michael, my name is Rebecca and this is Dr. Robert," Rebecca said as she walked over beside his bed.

"Hello Michael," Dr. Robert said.

"What can I do for you? Do you have some questions about the asylum?" Michael asked.

"We were looking through some of the old files and found a file with the name 'Sharon' on it and were wondering if you knew who Sharon was?" Rebecca asked.

"I haven't thought about Sharon for years," Michael replied, looking away like he was lost in thought.

"Do you know who she was, her last name or anything that can help us find out about her?" Dr. Robert asked.

"Yeah, I know who Sharon was. Her full name was Sharon Elizabeth Miller," Michael said.

"Miller, as in Michael Miller?" Dr. Robert asked.

"Yes, one in the same," Michael replied.

"Was she your wife?" Rebecca asked.

"Heavens no, she was my daughter," Michael said.

"Why does she have a file in the asylum records?" Dr. Robert asked.

"Well, the story actually starts back in the mid 1930's. There was a beautiful young girl named Elizabeth Joanne Parsons committed into the hospital by her father because he said she was possessed by the devil. I spent a great deal of time with her and never saw any signs of her being possessed. Sometimes during the nights the guards would report that she was acting strange and made up all kinds of crazy things - like her eyes were glowing or she floated in the air. I didn't believe any of their lies and we ended up getting married. We had a wonderful life together until we had our first child..."

"Sharon," Rebecca interrupted Michael.

"Yes, Sharon. She grew up like any normal child, the asylum became like a second home to her. Elizabeth had a problem with Sharon, though, and began resenting her. I never really knew what happened between them, but Elizabeth spoke to me several times about how evil Sharon was. Just before Sharon's eleventh birthday there was a horrible accident. My sweet Elizabeth took a terrible fall down the stairs and passed away. Sharon was home when it happened and found Elizabeth at the bottom of the stairs, that must have traumatized her," Michael said.

"Do you think that Sharon had something to do with Elizabeth falling?" Dr. Robert asked.

"No," Dr. Robert demanded. "Sharon didn't do a thing."

"What happened to Sharon?"

"As Sharon got older, we grew apart and she eventually became so sheltered that I ended up committing her in the asylum. I did not keep her files with the other patients though. I kept them in my personal files," Dr. Robert said.

"Is she in the new hospital?" Dr. Robert asked.

"No, I lost my Sharon to an awful accident at the asylum. One of the patients went totally off the wall and started killing people in the asylum. It was never determined which patient actually did the killing, but there were four patients and two guards killed during the situation. The nurses came in the following morning, and everyone on the wing was dead. It was awful," Michael concluded.

"That's a pretty amazing story," Rebecca said.

"I am sorry for your loss," Dr Robert said noticing the heartache in Michael's eyes.

"I'm OK. I have learned to live with the pain. Now that you have brought up all those painful memories, is there anything else you want to know about that old asylum?" Michael asked.

"Did you or any of your crew ever have any experiences that you could not explain?" Dr. Robert asked.

"What do you mean by 'experiences'?" Michael asked.

"You know, has anything happened that you can't explain?" Dr. Robert continued.

"Not really, maybe a couple of times in the tunnel, I got the creeps. But other than that no, Michael said.

"Tunnel, what tunnel?" Rebecca insisted.

"The tunnel that led from the asylum to the burial ground in the hill behind the asylum," Michael said.

"I have never seen a tunnel anywhere in the asylum," Rebecca said.

"You probably didn't see it because I had it disguised," Michael said.

"How did you disguise it?" Rebecca asked.

"In the basement, there is a set of double doors that lead into a broom closet," Michael said.

"I have been there," Rebecca said.

"I have too," Dr. Robert said.

"Then you have both been to the tunnel. Shortly after Sharon passed away my grief had overtaken my life and in my attempts to relieve the pain. I closed the tunnel. I merely had the maintenance men put in a wall to block the tunnel and make it into a room," Michael said.

"You mean the closet in the basement is actually a tunnel?" Rebecca asked.

"You mean that wall has not been torn down yet?" Michael asked.

"I was just there last week, and it still looks like a room," Dr. Robert said.

"I think that's the only questions we had. We appreciate your help," Rebecca said.

"Yeah, thanks for your help. We really do appreciate it," Dr. Robert said.

Dr. Robert and Rebecca turned for the door, and just before making it out the door Michael began speaking again.

"You know, I really didn't tell you the truth," Michael said.

Dr. Robert turned around and said, "What... what did you say?"

"I didn't tell you the whole truth. The part about the people dying is true but the where they actually died was not true. The incident actually happened in the tunnel. No one actually knows what happened, but it was terrible. I lost my little girl. It wasn't her fault it was the devil inside of her," Michael said.

"I'm sorry about Sharon," Dr. Robert said.

Dr. Robert and Rebecca walked out of Michael's house in amazement of the information they just learned. Both were anxious to get back to the asylum to try to disassemble the wall to look for the tunnel.

"Pull to the other end of the building and park near the whitewashed door," Rebecca told Dr. Robert as they pulled onto the asylum property. "That door goes into the stairway that will take us to the basement."

Dr. Robert and Rebecca got out of the car, walked to the door and Rebecca unlocked it. They walked through the door and headed down into the basement.

"I can't believe this tunnel has been here the whole time and I had no idea it was here," Rebecca said as she continued to walk through the rooms of the basement.

"That explains why Joey drew the picture that showed a tunnel, and if Sharon actually died in the tunnel that may explain why he saw her there," Dr. Robert said.

"It's right over here," Rebecca said, leading Dr. Robert through the double door.

"How are we going to get through the wall?" Dr. Robert asked.

"I don't know, maybe we should..." Rebecca said as she picked up a sledge hammer and slammed it into the wall.

"I think I'm getting your point," Dr. Robert said as he picked up a sledge hammer and also began slamming it into the wall.

After several swings of the sledge hammer, the wall started to slowly fall back away from where they where standing.

"I think it's going to fall," Dr Robert said as he stopped swinging.

The wall slowly started falling, and then without resistance, it slammed onto the floor. Dust flew from around the wall when it hit the floor causing Dr. Robert and Rebecca to quickly cover their mouths. They both stood still for several minutes, waiting for the dust to settle and trying to see through the darkness down the tunnel. The darkness filled the air and let no light into the tunnel.

"I don't think this tunnel comes out anywhere, do you?" Dr. Robert asked.

"I don't know. Are there lights anywhere?" Rebecca said.

"I don't see any," Dr. Robert said.

"We're going to have to find some flashlights or something before we go on," Rebecca said.

"OK, but we need to secure the doors before we leave," Dr. Robert said.

Dr. Robert and Rebecca both stepped back and pulled the door shut behind them. Rebecca used her keys to lock the door.

"The only other person who has a key to this door is Charlie, and he won't be back until next week," Rebecca said.

"Good, no one will get in there until we can get our supplies," Dr. Robert said.

Dr. Robert and Rebecca worked their way back out of the basement, up the stairs and back out to where Dr. Robert's car was parked.

"It is starting to get late. Do you think we should make a plan and come back in the morning?" Rebecca asked.

"I don't have any supplies, so I don't have a problem with starting first thing in the morning," Dr. Robert said.

"That's fine, I'll take the files and make a copy of them for you and meet you back here around nine in the morning?" Rebecca suggested.

"OK, I will bring some flashlights and I think I will bring my video camera too," Dr. Robert said.

"I'll see you in the morning," Rebecca said as she walked away from Dr. Robert's car.

Dr. Robert got into his car and began the drive back to his house in Deerfield. His imagination ran wild with what could be in the tunnel and the adventure he had found himself in.

Chapter Eleven

Exploring the Tunnel

The following morning Dr. Robert woke up early and prepared supplies to navigate through the tunnel. He found an old handgun that his father had given him and stuffed it into a backpack in case of wild animals. He felt like a child preparing for his first day of school. He loaded his equipment into his car and just as he was getting ready to leave, he noticed that someone had left him a message.

"Dr. Robert, this is Sue. Joey has not been doing so well since he visited the asylum. He is having nightmares every night and wakes up screaming the name 'Sharon'. Could you call me so we can talk," the recording said.

Dr. Robert thought about whether he was going to return her call now or wait until he returned. After a long period of consideration, he decided to wait until he returned from the asylum. Dr. Robert finished packing his car and headed for the asylum.

"This place amazes me every time I see it," he said out loud to himself as he pulled into the parking lot. Rebecca was standing at the front entrance of the asylum waiting for Dr. Robert to park.

"Good morning," Dr. Robert said as he got out of his car.

"Good morning. Are you ready to explore?" Rebecca said.

"Ready as I'll ever be," Dr. Robert said as he unloaded his supplies from his car.

Walking to the entrance of the asylum where Rebecca was standing Dr. Robert asked, "Are you ready to explore?"

"I'm a little freaked out, but I wouldn't miss this for the world," Rebecca said.

Dr. Robert stepped in the front door and looked around, thinking of whom or what may be watching him in the foyer. Rebecca stepped inside behind him and also cautiously looked around.

"Feels different since Joey was here, doesn't it?" Dr. Robert asked.

"Yeah, I get cold chills every time I walk in the door now," Rebecca said.

"I brought two flashlights, a digital voice recorder and a video recorder," Dr. Robert said.

"Are those standard psychiatrist tools?" Rebecca jokingly asked.

"No, just things I have accumulated over the years," Dr. Robert replied.

"I know, I was just giving you a hard time," Rebecca replied.

"Here's your flashlight," Dr. Robert said, handing it to Rebecca.

"Thanks," Rebecca replied.

"Will you hold on to this digital recorder for me so I can video?" Dr. Robert asked.

"Sure," Rebecca said, taking the recorder from Dr. Robert's hand.

Dr. Robert finished gathering his equipment and then tested his video recorder to make sure the battery was charged.

"Are you ready?" Rebecca asked.

"Yeah, everything is in working order, and I am ready to roll," Dr. Robert said as he started to walk down the hall.

Rebecca walked ahead, leading Dr. Robert down the hall and into the stairway. Reaching the basement they walked at a slow pace, but the deeper they walked into the basement the harder their breathing became.

"I must have been blinded by the excitement last night because today I'm afraid," Rebecca said.

"I am too. The unknown is always scary," Dr. Robert replied as he continued to walk through the basement until he finally reached the entrance to the tunnel room.

Rebecca stops at the door and looks back at Dr. Robert, "Are you ready?"

"I'm ready if you are! Turn on your recorder," Dr. Robert said, turning on his video camera.

Dr. Robert stepped into the room and flipped the light switch on. The light lit up the first ten feet or so, but beyond that, it was pitch black. The wall was still on the floor and the odor of mildew and mold reeked throughout the air. Dr. Robert stepped cautiously through room until he reached the darkness and began scanning the area, looking for anything and looking at everything. He held his flashlight in his left hand but was also using the light on the video camera in his right hand. Rebecca walked close behind Dr. Robert and used her flashlight to help scan through the darkness.

"Help me! Get me out of here!" Rebecca started screaming and grabbing at Dr. Robert as her voice echoed through the tunnel.

"What? What is it?" Dr. Robert yelled back at Rebecca.

"Help me! You gotta get me out of here!" Rebecca continued to yell at Dr. Robert.

"I can't help you if I don't know what happened," Dr. Robert said and then noticed a large sewer rat moving along the wall. "Is that it?" he began laughing.

"It's not funny. Get me out of here," Rebecca said, still screaming.

"Listen, that little rat is not going to eat you. You need to relax so we can move on," Dr. Robert said.

"Get it away from me," Rebecca said, still panicking.

"That rat is ten feet from you. Just relax and it will eventually go away," Dr. Robert said as he pulled Rebecca's hands loose from his arms.

"OK, OK, it's leaving," Rebecca said, calming down.

Being only a few feet into the tunnel, Dr. Robert began looking around the tunnel to make sure the structure would hold up. The tunnel was arch shaped made of large stones with a floor made with old brick that was laid in a random pattern. There were random puddles of water and small drips of water falling from roots that stuck down through the cracks between the stones in the upper part of the arch. The tunnel let no traces of light in, so the flashlights only cut through about ten to fifteen feet of the darkness. The bricks on the floor had a slight film of mud covering them, but it was not thick enough to make them slide.

"Are you ready to go?" Dr. Robert asked.

"I guess so, but I really don't like rats," Rebecca replied.

"I can tell," Dr. Robert said as he turned his light back down the tunnel.

They began walking in the tunnel, looking all around for anything that could lead to the mystery of the tunnel. They continued to walk for several hundred feet and had not seen anything strange or out of place.

"How far have we gone?" Rebecca asked.

"I think the question is, how far we are going to go?" Dr. Robert asked.

"Can you see the end yet?" Rebecca asked.

"No, I don't see anything that even resembles the end," Dr. Robert said as they continued to walk in a more relaxed posture through the tunnel.

"Maybe we should head back," Rebecca said.

"We have come this far, we..." Dr. Robert stopped talking.

"What is it?" Rebecca pointed her flashlight toward Dr. Roberts.

"Look," he said pointing his flashlight down the tunnel. His light was focused on black steel poles that led from ceiling to floor forming a barrier with a gate cut out in the middle.

"Why would they have a gate in a tunnel?" Dr. Robert asked.

"I don't know, maybe it's the end," Rebecca replied.

Dr. Robert walked up to the gate and grabbed the handle. Pulling several times he said, "I don't think it's locked."

"Why won't it open?" Rebecca asked.

"I think it is just rusted shut," Dr Robert said, putting the light and video camera on the floor, so he could pull with both hands.

"It moved," Rebecca said, keeping her light on the gate. Rebecca put her light on the floor and grabbed the gate to help him pull it open.

"Got it," Dr. Robert said as the door opened. Dr. Robert and Rebecca stood up and picked up their lights and recorder.

"I'll go first," Dr. Robert said as he moved around the gate to the doorway. He stepped over a metal beam and onto the floor on the other side. As soon as his body crossed the bar, the light on the video camera went out.

"What the heck?" Dr. Robert asked himself looking at the video camera. He shook it and then banged the side.

"I think the battery is dead," Rebecca said.

"It had a full battery just a few seconds ago," Dr. Robert said.

Dr. Robert messed with the video camera another minute and then said, "Oh, well, I guess I won't videotape anymore." He put the video camera strap over his shoulder and stepped further down the tunnel. Rebecca stepped through the gate and remained close to Dr. Robert. It appeared as though the structure of the bricks on the floor, had changed and was beginning to take form. The bricks started to form an aisle down the middle of the floor creating a walkway.

"Why can't we see the light at the end of the tunnel?" Rebecca said.

"I'm starting to think this is not a tunnel," Dr. Robert said.

"Why do you think that?" Rebecca asked.

"We have headed straight back into the hill. We have not gone toward the surface at all," Dr. Robert said.

"That makes sense, but if it doesn't come out somewhere, then where does it go?" Rebecca asked.

"I don't know where it goes, but I'm going to find out," Dr. Robert said as he continued to slowly navigate down the tunnel.

They followed the tunnel back another thirty feet, and Dr. Robert observed, "Hey, the tunnel is opening."

"What is it?" Rebecca said, shining her flashlight past him.

"It appears to be an old well." Dr. Robert said looking at a large circular stone structure that was two-foot tall wall and was open in the middle. The sidewalk split and was about three feet wide, surrounding the well.

"I wonder if this used to be the water supply for the asylum?" Rebecca asked.

"I don't know. I can't see anything in the bottom, it is too deep," Dr. Robert said. He took off his pack and pulled out a glow stick.

"What are you doing?" Rebecca asked.

"I am going to activate this glow stick and drop it into the well. We'll be able to see how far down the water is," Dr. Robert replied as he snapped the glow stick, lighting up the entire area where they were standing.

"Here goes nothing," Dr. Robert said dropping the glow stick into the well. It fell for fifteen to twenty feet and then it crashed into the bottom. "Holy smokes," he said in awe as he looked down into the well.

"What is it? What do you see?" Rebecca said anxiously.

"You don't want to know," Dr. Robert replied as he continued to stare into the hole.

"I have to look now," Rebecca said, stepping closer to the edge of the well. "What is it, I can't make it out."

"Look close," Dr. Robert said in a strange tone.

"'Aah!" Rebecca screamed realizing that what she was looking at was an array of human bones piled deep into the well. She identified skulls and rib cages laying scattered one on top of the other.

"I guess this tunnel did not lead to a cemetery, but to more of a dumping ground for bodies," Dr. Robert concluded.

"Who would do such a thing? Why would they do this?" Rebecca asked, moving away from the well.

"They were probably hiding the bodies. If they did experimental surgeries and all the things you say they did, they did not want anyone to see what they were doing, so they hid them here," Dr. Robert said.

"I'm getting out of here," Rebecca said waiting for Dr. Robert to respond.

"I think we should go back and talk to Michael Miller. He seems to have forgotten to tell us some things about the tunnel," Dr. Robert said.

Dr. Robert and Rebecca turn and walked back toward the exit. The gravity of what they had seen still echoing in their head.

Chapter Twelve

Joey's Past

Dr. Robert and Rebecca reached the outside of the asylum and stood for a minute waiting for their eyes to adjust to the sunshine. As the thought of the horrifying sight still echoed in their minds, they did not speak.

Finally Dr. Robert looked over at Rebecca and said, "I think we definitely need to talk to Michael again. Maybe he wasn't as truthful as he could have been."

"I agree, but I can't do it today. What are you doing in the morning?" Rebecca said.

"That's fine. I need to go back and talk to Joey." Thinking for a minute, he continued, "why don't we just wait a couple days so I can try to figure out what is going on with Joey," he said.

"That's good for me. I'll have Charlie go down and secure that door," Rebecca said.

Dr. Robert arrived back in at his residence late in the evening. When he walked in the house, he saw there was a message on his answering machine.

"Dr. Robert, this is Sue again. I really need to talk to you. Joey is worse and we need your advice on what to do. We're not getting any sleep, and Joey is exhausted. Please give me a call back. Thank you."

Dr. Robert stopped unpacking his equipment and opened his Rolodex for Sue's phone number. He found the number, sat the book down and dialed her number.

"Hello," Sue answered the phone.

"Sue, this is Dr. Robert. What's going on?"

"Thank goodness. Joey has barely slept since he went to that asylum. What happened there?" Sue asked.

"Not much really. He said he saw some things, but there was nothing dramatic that should have upset him," Dr. Robert replied.

"He did not sleep at all last night, every time he closes his eyes he begins to scream," Sue said.

"Can he come back to my office tomorrow?" Dr. Robert asked.

"Yes, what time?" Sue asked.

"What time does he get out of school?" Dr. Robert asked.

"I am not sending him to school. He's exhausted," Sue said.

"If he isn't going to school, then why don't you have him here at nine," Dr. Robert replied.

"That would be great. I'll see you in the morning," Sue was relieved.

"OK, bye," Dr. Robert said, hanging up the phone.

The following morning just before nine, Sue and Joey showed up at Dr. Robert's office.

"Hello," Sue said, walking into an empty waiting room.

"Hello," Dr. Robert's voice came from the back of the building.

"It's Sue and Joey!" Sue yelled.

"Hello Sue. Hello Joey," Dr. Robert said. "Joey, are you ready to come back?"

"Yeah," Joey said, as he stood up and walked to the door leading to the back.

"Are you going to wait or do you want me to give you a call when we're done?" Dr. Robert asked Sue.

"I think, if you don't mind, I will run over to the book store," Sue said.

"That'll be fine. I'll call you if you're not back by the time we're done," Dr. Robert said.

"OK," Sue said as she picked up her purse and walked out the door.

Dr. Robert followed Joey back to the office where Joey climbed up into the chair.

"So, your mom tells me that you have had some bad nights?" Dr. Robert asked.

"Yes, I've been having nightmares," Joey said.

"How many nightmares have you had?" Dr. Robert asked.

"Every night since we went to the asylum," Joey said.

"What are you dreaming about?" Dr. Robert asked.

Joey put his head down and quietly muttered, "Sharon."

"Sharon, what's she doing?" Dr. Robert asked.

"She's in my dreams," Joey said.

"What's she doing?" Dr. Robert asked.

"She is pulling me to the tunnel," Joey replied.

"Why?" Dr. Robert asked.

"I don't know," Joey replied.

"Tell me exactly what happens," Dr. Robert asked.

"It starts with me walking into the building and I see Sharon standing in front of me. I try to run, but she grabs my arm and tries to drag me to the tunnel," Joey said.

"What makes you think she is trying to take you to the tunnel?" Dr. Robert asked.

"The first time I dreamed about Sharon I walked into the basement with her. It was dark and I was scared. I walked to the entrance of the tunnel with her, and she looked back at me and her eyes turned red. I tried to run, but she grabbed me and started dragging me toward the tunnel. I fought and screamed until I woke up," Joey explained.

"Is that what happens every time?" Dr. Robert asked.

"Most of the time. When I see her, I try to get out of the building, but she always grabs me and tries to pull me inside," Dr. Robert said.

"Has she ever said anything to you?" Dr. Robert asked.

"Yeah, when she grabs me, she starts saying 'You must see' over and over," Joey said.

"What is she talking about when she says you must see?" Dr. Robert asked.

"I don't know. I don't want to go to the tunnel and see," Joey explained.

"Let's get off this subject and let me ask some routine questions." Dr. Robert said.

"OK," Joey replied.

"Where were you born?" Dr. Robert asked.

"I don't know," Joey replied.

"Has your mom ever told you where you were born?" Dr. Robert asked.

"I don't know my mother," Joey said.

"What about Sue?" Dr. Robert asked, thinking Joey was just playing a game.

"Sue is not my mom. She is my adopted mom," Joey said.

"Oh, I didn't know that," Dr. Robert said.

"Yeah, I was a baby. They told me when I was old enough to understand," Joey said.

"Do you know anything about your real parents?" Dr. Robert asked.

"No, just that Joseph is my real name, and I think they told me that my real dads name is Joseph too," Joey said.

"Do you know where you were born?" Dr. Robert asked.

"No," Joey replied.

"Would you mind if I asked Sue about your real parents?" Dr. Robert asked.

"You can ask her, and it's OK to call her my mom. Even though she is not my real mom, she is the only mom I know," Joey explained.

"Would you mind if I went and checked to see if your mom is out in the waiting room?" Dr. Robert asked.

"OK, I'll wait here," Joey said.

Dr. Robert walked out the door and into the waiting room. Sue was sitting in the waiting room reading a book when Dr. Robert walked in.

"Sue," Dr. Robert said.

"Yes," Sue replied.

"Would you mind walking back here with me for a minute?" Dr. Robert asked.

"Sure. Is everything all right?" Sue asked.

"Everything is fine. We just wanted to ask you some questions," Dr. Robert said.

"OK," Sue said as she walked back to Dr. Robert's office.

"Hey buddy, how's it going?" Sue asked Joey as she walked in the office.

"Good," Joey replied.

"Sue, Joey has confided in me the fact that he was adopted, but he does not know anything about his past. I was wondering if you could help me out and tell me about his family history." Dr. Robert asked.

"Well, we adopted Joey when he was one month old. Unfortunately, Joey's mother died when she was giving birth to him. Joey's father was listed on the birth certificate but I don't think he ever knew that Joey was his child. I think Joey's mother decided not to tell him that she was pregnant," Sue said.

"Do you know what Joey's mom and dad's names were," Dr. Robert asked.

"I think that's his Dad's name was Joseph McCall, and his Mom's name was Lori Miller," Sue answered.

"Miller? Are you sure her name was Miller?" Dr. Robert asked, remembering that the administrator of the asylum was Miller.

"Yeah, I'm certain her name was Miller," Sue replied.

"Do you know anything else about the parents or grandparents?" Dr. Robert asked.

"Not really. I think that there was a grandfather, but he was widowed and could not take care of the child, so Social Services took the child," Sue said.

"So do you know anything about the medical history of Joey?" Dr. Robert asked.

"I only know since birth, Social Services told me that they didn't know any other medical information on the family," Sue said.

"I'm trying to find a connection between Joey and the asylum and finding out that his last name is Miller, it looks like he may be related to the old administrator," Dr. Robert said.

"Do you think Joey has some type of mental illness because of who he is related to?" Sue asked.

"It's possible, but I don't think that Joey has a mental illness, I think he is related to he person named 'Sharon' in his dreams," Dr. Robert said.

"Joey, do you know this Sharon woman?" Sue asked Joey, who had not told his mother about his dreams.

"Yeah," Joey said.

"Joey, do you want me to explain your dreams to your mom? If you don't want me to tell, I won't or if you want to tell her you can," Dr. Robert explained.

"It's OK," Joey said, looking at his mom. "I have dreams about the asylum and I meet people in there. Most people are nice to me, but there is a woman named 'Sharon' that scares me."

"What does she do?" Sue asked.

"She tries to take me into a tunnel, and it's really scary," Joey explained.

"Does she hurt you?" Sue asked, getting concerned for Joey's well-being.

"No Mom, she is in my dream," Joey reassured his mom.

"Sue, there is something drawing Joey to the asylum. Even though he sees a few different people when he goes there, in his dreams it could be just one spirit calling him. My guess is that Sharon is the one getting him there, and the other spirits are using him while he is there," Dr. Robert said.

"Using him? What do you mean using him?" Sue asked.

"They use his energy to form into physical form. It doesn't hurt him," Dr. Robert explained.

"Is there any way to stop his bad dreams?" Sue asked.

"I've been working on stopping them, but I think that Joey is going to have to go with Sharon into the tunnel," Dr. Robert said.

"No," Joey insisted.

"It's OK honey. If you don't want to go with her you don't have to," Sue replied.

"She's right Joey. You don't have to do anything but we are going to have to try some things to help you get rid of the bad dreams," Dr. Robert said.

"I'm afraid of her," Joey said.

"Let's take one step at a time. I will start trying to find out a little bit about Joey's past. I'll call you in a couple days and we can meet again," Dr. Robert said.

"What do we do if Joey continues to have bad dreams?" Sue asked.

"I'm sorry, but I have not figured that out yet. Maybe if I can figure out the connection, I can break it," Dr. Robert said.

"OK, we'll wait for your call," Sue replied.

"Bye Dr. Robert," Joey said.

Chapter Thirteen

Joey's Family History

The next morning Dr. Robert called Rebecca.

"Trans Allegheny Lunatic Asylum, this is Rebecca. How may I help you?" Rebecca answered the phone.

"Rebecca, this is Dr. Robert," Dr. Robert said.

"Hey, how are you doing?" Rebecca asked.

"I'm doing great. How are you?" Dr. Robert asked.

"I'm good, just waiting to hear when we're going to finish our ghost hunt," Rebecca said.

"I'm getting closer to heading back into the tunnel, but I think we may need to go back and talk to Michael Miller first," Dr. Robert said.

"Ask him about the tunnel?" Rebecca asked.

"Yeah, the tunnel and the fact that I found out that Joey's real last name is Miller," Dr. Robert said.

"Are you kidding? Joey may be related to Michael Miller?" Rebecca asked.

"I don't know, it would explain the connection between the asylum and Joey," Dr. Robert said.

"That would make sense," Rebecca said.

"Are you available to meet me this afternoon to go to Michael Miller's house?" Dr. Robert asked.

"Sure. Do you want me to call him?" Rebecca replied.

"I don't think he will mind us just showing up. It didn't appear as though he had a busy schedule," Dr. Robert said.

"That sounds fine, just pull around the asylum to the office. I'll watch for you," Rebecca said.

"I will see you in a few hours, bye," Dr. Robert said.

"Bye," Rebecca replied.

Dr. Robert went to his office and laid out Joey's file. He decided to go through the file and make a list of questions that he would like answered, some that he expected Michael Miller to answer and others he did not know who could answer. Dr. Robert finished his list and then tried to figure out some possible scenarios that would connect Joey to the asylum. Realizing that Joey was only around nine years old, it would make it impossible for him to have a relationship with Sharon. He thought about possible relationships with Michael Miller and that fact he was so old, it was hard to put a relationship between them. Dr. Robert decided to stop worrying about the possible relationship, gathered the file and neatly tucked it under his arm. He went to his car and drove to the asylum. He pulled into the asylum parking lot, pulled around the building and parked in front of the office door. Dr. Robert stepped out of the car and looks up and saw Rebecca coming out of the door.

"Hey," Rebecca said.

"Hey, what's up?" Dr. Robert asked as he stretched.

"Same old stuff," Rebecca said.

"If you're ready, we can go ahead over to Michael's house," Dr. Robert said.

"That's fine with me," Rebecca said as she walked to Dr. Robert's car and sat in the passenger seat.

Dr. Robert got back into his car and began the short drive to Michael Miller's house. Pulling in front of the house, Dr. Robert and Rebecca got out of the car and walked to the front door. After ringing the doorbell, Dr. Robert and Rebecca waited patiently for someone to answer the door.

"Hello" Sandy said, opening the door.

"Hello, we were here the other day," Rebecca began to explain.

"I remember you Rebecca, and how are you, Dr. Robert?" Sandy said.

"I'm fine, thanks for asking," Dr. Robert said.

"Come on in," Sandy said.

Dr. Robert and Rebecca stepped into the house and waited for Sandy to shut the door.

"Are you here to talk to Michael?" Sandy said.

"If he's not busy we would like to ask him a couple of questions," Dr. Robert asked.

"He hasn't been out of bed in two years, I'm sure he's not busy," Sandy said as she led them toward Michael's room.

"Michael, you have visitors," Sandy said.

"Michael quickly looked up and said "Dr. Robert, Rebecca, how are you?"

"We're fine, Michael. How are you?" Dr. Robert said.

"I suppose you have some questions for me?" Michael said.

"How did you know that?" Rebecca said.

"I can only guess that you went down to the tunnel and discovered that it's not really a tunnel," Michael said.

"Yeah, and not only that, but about what we found at the end of the passage," Dr. Robert said.

"You don't understand. When I ran the asylum times were tough. I had to take every person that wanted to be there and every person the state ordered to be there," Michael said.

"Why would you do that to those people? They were human beings," Rebecca said.

"Human beings? I treated those people better than most of their families did. The families dropped them off and never came back, not even to visit. They abandoned them, left them there to die. I treated them like they were all one big family, I gave them a home and love," Michael explained.

"Why did you just throw their bodies away like trash? You didn't even give them a proper burial," Rebecca said, getting upset.

"It was really an easy choice," Michael said.

"What's so easy about discarding a human's life," Dr. Robert said.

"I had a memorial service for every person who passed away at the asylum, the body was just their physical form. Times got so hard that I had to choose whether I was going to properly bury the dead patients or buy food for the patients that were still alive. It was not a choice I took lightly, but I had to do what I had to," Michael explained.

"I'm sorry I got upset, I had no idea," Rebecca said.

"It wasn't an easy decision, but when I figured out how much money I would save by disposing of the bodies myself, it made it easy. I just had to figure out how to hide them," Michael explained.

"So you dug a passage into the hill and dug a deep hole to dispose of the bodies," Dr. Robert said, finishing the statement that Michael had started.

"I buried my own daughter there. It wasn't a bad place. A person should be remembered for what they did in life, not where they were buried," Michael said.

"OK, I don't like what you did but I understand why you did it. Let me change the subject, I have found a little boy with the last name of Miller. He was adopted because the mother died at birth," Dr. Robert said.

"Joey?" Michael asked.

"How did you know?" Dr. Robert asked.

"Where is he? Can I see him?" Michael said.

"First you have to tell me what you know about him?" Dr. Robert said.

"After I lost Elizabeth and Sharon, I was devastated, but then I met another woman, a nurse at the asylum named Tonya. I married her, and we had a child named Lori who was a bright beautiful girl. Tonya gave birth to her at the asylum. Unfortunately, I lost Tonya to the flu, and me and Lori grew apart. When she was sixteen, she ran away and never came home. I reported her missing to the police, but they had too much to do and never found her. I hired a private investigator to find her several years later, and they found her just before having her baby. I saw the birth announcement of Joey and the obituary of Lori. The paper only comes out once a week, and when the paper came out I went to the hospital. When I got to the hospital, they told me that Social Services took the child and they told me the only way I could see my daughter is by talking to the coroner. I did talk to the coroner and was able to give this daughter a proper burial. I talked to a nurse later that said the child was given the name Joseph before Lori had passed away - that is all the information I had," Michael explained.

"That explains the connection. Joey is actually Sharon's nephew," Dr. Robert said.

"Explains what connection?" Michael asked.

"I have met with Joey, and he is having dreams about Sharon. Joey lives in Deerfield with a nice family," Dr. Robert said.

"Can I meet him?" Michael said.

"We can talk about that later. I will try to set up a meeting between you and his parents. There is a little more to the story - Sharon is trying to take Joey down into the tunnel in his dreams," Dr. Robert said.

"What does she want?" Michael asked.

"I haven't figured it out yet, but I think I can start piecing it together. I appreciate your time. You have given us a wealth of information," Dr. Robert said as he stood up and walked toward the door.

Rebecca stood up behind him and said, "Good bye Michael."

"If you need anything else, just come over," Michael said.

They arrived at the car, and before getting in, Dr. Robert looked over the roof at Rebecca and said, "What do you think?"

"I don't know. This situation is getting stranger the more we get into it," Rebecca said.

"I know. It's like we were only getting part of the story, and now it's all falling into place," Dr. Robert said as he sat down in the car.

Rebecca sat down in the passenger seat and asked, "What now?"

"I think I should go back and meet with Joey and his mother and explain that Sharon is related to them. Maybe I can convince him to talk to Sharon," Dr. Robert said.

"What about all the bodies in that tunnel?" Rebecca asked.

"I don't know what to do about them, I guess you could either give them a proper burial or just fill in the hole with dirt and forget about them," Dr. Robert said.

"I will never forget about them, the image is burned in my brain. I might just fill in the hole and make a memorial for them somewhere on the asylum grounds," Rebecca said.

Dr. Robert drove Rebecca to the asylum office and said, "I will call you tonight or in the morning and let you know what's going on," he said.

"OK," Rebecca said, stepping out of the car.

Dr. Robert returned to his office and made a small genealogical tree to explain to Sue and Joey why he felt Sharon was appearing in his dreams. He decided to meet with Joey the following day and called Sue to make arrangements.

"Hello," Sue answered.

"Hello, Sue, this is Dr. Robert," he answered.

"Hello Dr. Robert, what's the good news?" Sue asked.

"I actually found some interesting information. I was wondering if you could bring Joey over in the morning so we can talk?" Dr. Robert asked.

"I haven't sent him to school since this whole thing started, so I can have him over there as early as you need us." Sue replied.

"Great, how about nine?" Dr. Robert asked.

"OK I will see you then. Goodbye," Sue said.

"Bye," Dr. Robert replied.

Chapter Fourteen

Back to the Asylum

The following morning just before nine, Sue walked in the door with Joey close behind her. There was no receptionist, so Sue yelled through the door, "Hello."

"Hello, come on back," Dr. Robert yelled from his office.

Sue and Joey walked back to Dr. Robert's office and stepped inside.

"Good morning, how are we doing today?" Dr. Robert asked as Joey climbed into the chair and Sue stood beside him.

"Tired, we didn't get much sleep last night, but we're OK," Sue answered.

"Joey, how are you doing?" Dr. Robert asked.

"I'm OK," Joey replied.

"Joey, do you mind if Mommy sits with us while we talk?" Dr. Robert asked.

"No, she can stay," Joey replied.

"Tell me what happened last night," Dr. Robert said to Joey.

"I had a bad dream," Joey said.

"Tell me what happened," Dr. Robert said.

"I went to the building and Sharon was there. I walked to the tunnel with her and her eyes turned red and scared me, so I ran away," Joey said.

"Did you see anything in the tunnel?" Dr. Robert asked.

"No, as soon as we got to the tunnel, her eyes got red. It was dark in the tunnel," Joey said.

"Did she try to stop you from running away?" Dr. Robert asked.

"She grabbed my arm," Joey said.

"Which arm?" Dr. Robert asked.

"This one," Joey said, holding up his right arm which had finger shaped bruises on it.

"What happened to your arm?" Sue asked in a scared tone.

"She grabbed me," Joey said.

Noticing how upset Sue was getting, Dr. Robert decided to get into Joey's family history.

"Sue, I found out a little bit about Joey's past. His mother's name was Lori Miller and she died giving birth to Joey. Joey's grandfather is a man named Michael Miller, and he lives in Weston," Dr. Robert explained.

"He's alive? Why didn't he want Joey?" Sue said.

"Lori and Michael got into an argument and Lori ran off when she was sixteen. By the time Michael learned she had a child, the child had been adopted. Michael tried to get Social Services to give him Joey but they had no proof that Lori was his daughter or Joey was his grandson," Dr. Robert explained.

"What about birth certificates or hospital records?" Sue asked.

"Unfortunately for Michael, Lori was born in the asylum and there were no records generated," Dr. Robert explained.

"Do you believe him?" Sue asked.

"Yes, because it establishes the link between Sharon and Joey," Dr. Robert said.

"What link?" Sue asked.

"Michael had two children. Lori, who had Joey, and a child named Sharon. Besides Michael Miller, the only living relative to Sharon would be Joey," Dr. Robert said.

"What does she want from Joey?" Sue asked.

"Does that mean Sharon is my aunt?" Joey interjected.

"Yes, Sharon would be your aunt," Dr. Robert said.

"Why is she in my dreams?" Joey asked.

"I don't know what she wants. Now that you know she is your aunt, would you feel better about trying to talk to her?" Dr. Robert asked.

"I... don't know," Joey hesitated.

"The only way we are going to stop the bad dreams is if you talk to Sharon in your dream, or you go back to the asylum and talk to her there," Dr. Robert said.

"Is that the only way?" Sue asked.

"I don't know - I don't even know if it will help. Joey's case is unprecedented and I have nothing to base my diagnosis on," Dr. Robert said.

"Joey, do you think you can handle this?" Sue said.

"I don't know. She scares me every night, and I don't want to have any more bad dreams," Joey replied.

"Joey, do you want to go back to the asylum and try to face Sharon with us?" Dr. Robert asked.

"Will it make my dreams stop?" Joey asked.

"I think it will," Dr. Robert said.

"I think we should go, Mom," Joey said looking at his Mom.

"I'll go only if you want me to go," Sue said.

"I'll call a friend of mine and see when we can go," Dr. Robert said as he stood up and walked out the door. He walked to the front office and called Rebecca on the phone.

"Trans-Allegheny Lunatic Asylum, this is Rebecca. How may I help you?" Rebecca said.

"Rebecca, this is Dr. Robert. I talked to Joey and his mother, and they agreed to come to the asylum to try to find out why Sharon is in his dreams."

"That's great! When are you coming over?" Rebecca asked.

"I was just checking to see when you would be available. We can be there today at one, if that's OK with you," Dr. Robert asked.

"That'll be fine. I'll be waiting for you in my office," Rebecca said.

"OK, bye," Dr. Robert said.

Dr. Robert walked back into his office, "Sue, I talked to my friend Rebecca, and she will be there all day. Do you want to try to go there this afternoon?" Dr. Robert asked.

"Sure, I have to stop by the house and call my husband. I think the sooner we can go down there the better off we will be," Sue said.

"OK, I need to get some stuff ready and meet you back here around noon. You can park at my office and I'll drive us to the asylum," Dr. Robert said.

"That's fine. I'll see you around noon," Sue said, as she and Joey stood and headed out the door.

"Bye Dr. Robert," Joey said as he left the room.

"See you in a little bit, Joey," Dr. Robert said.

After Sue and Joey left, Dr. Robert sat down and tried to work out a plan on what to do with Joey in the event that Sharon took him. He decided that the best way to keep Joey close to him was to tie a rope around his waist and keep it tight. He decided that if anything got Joey, they would have to get him also.

Just after noon, Sue and Joey pulled into the Dr. Robert's office parking lot and parked close to the entrance.

"I'm sorry we're late, I tried to run too many errands," Sue explained.

"No problem, we have plenty of time," Dr. Robert reassured her.

"Hey Dr. Robert," Joey said.

"Hey Joey, how's it going?" Dr. Robert asked.

"Fine," Joey replied.

"If you're ready to go, we will get going," Dr. Robert said.

Dr. Robert, Sue and Joey climbed into Dr. Robert's car and headed for the asylum.

"How far is it?" Sue asked.

"About thirty minutes," Dr. Robert answered.

"Is Rebecca going to be there?" Joey asked.

"Yes, she will," Dr. Roberts replied. "Are you ready to talk to Sharon?"

"Yes, I guess," Joey said.

"How will we know if Sharon is even there?" Sue asked.

"Joey is the only one that will know if she is there," Dr. Robert said.

"How will he know," Sue asked.

"We will walk with him into the entrance of the asylum. She should meet us there. Joey will be able to see her and tell us what she is doing," Dr. Robert said.

"What if she doesn't show up?" Sue asked.

"She is using his dreams to pull him to the asylum, she will not pass this opportunity up," Dr. Robert explained.

The conversation faded off and Sue gazed off, lost in her own thoughts. Joey played in the back seat with his seatbelt. Dr. Robert sat quietly and concentrated on trying not to get overly anxious.

Arriving in front of the building Sue read the sign, "Trans-Allegheny Lunatic Asylum, what a huge building."

"They don't build buildings like this anymore, do they?" Dr. Robert asked.

"No, they sure don't," Sue said.

Dr. Robert pulled around the building to the office entrance and parked. "This is it," he said.

Dr. Robert, Sue and Joey got out of the car and walked into Rebecca's office.

"Hello?" Dr. Robert yelled.

"Hey," Rebecca said as she walked into her office.

"Sue this is Rebecca. Her family owns the asylum. Rebecca, this is Sue, Joey's mom, and of course, you remember Joey?" Dr. Robert asked.

"Nice to meet you, Sue," Rebecca said as they shook hands.

"You too," Sue replied.

"Hey Joey, of course I remember you," Rebecca said, touching Joey on the head.

"What do we need?" Dr. Robert asked Rebecca.

"I gathered some supplies that my dad uses for camping that should help us. I got two lanterns, a couple flashlights, and this pellet gun, just in case we see any unwanted visitors," Rebecca said.

"The lanterns will help. Does your dad have a climbing rope?" Dr. Robert asked.

"I think so, let me check," Rebecca said as she walked out of the room. Returning a few minutes later, she came back in the room carrying a black climbing rope, "How about this?"

"That will work great. I think that's all we need," Dr. Robert said.

"OK, we can walk through the building to get to the basement," Rebecca said.

"I don't think we can do that. I think we will have to walk in the front entrance," Dr. Robert said.

"OK, let's walk out around the building and we will go in the front door," Rebecca said.

"Why the front entrance?" Sue asked.

"Joey's point of contact with these spirits is the front entrance," Dr. Robert said.

"What do these spirits look like?" Sue asked.

"Joey is the only one who can see them, so I really don't know exactly what they look like." Dr. Robert said.

"Joey, are they scary?" Sue asked.

"No, they just look like people," Joey replied.

As they approached the front entrance, Dr. Robert said, "Let's get ready because if Sharon is waiting for us, we should be prepared to follow her."

Rebecca set the lanterns on the ground and started working on lighting them. Dr. Robert prepared the rope and wrapped it around the waist of Joey, securing it to his own waist too.

"What's that for?" Sue asked.

"I don't think anything will happen, but if it does, I want to make sure Joey is safe," Dr. Robert said.

"Here," Rebecca said handing Dr. Robert a lantern.

"OK, Joey, if you're ready to go, we'll head inside," Dr. Robert said.

"I'm ready," Joey said.

Dr. Robert opened the door and let Joey walk in the door in front of him. "Is she here?" Dr. Robert asked.

"Yeah, she's right there," Joey said pointing toward the corner of the foyer.

"Where is she?" Sue asked anxiously.

"Right there, Mom," Joey said pointing to the same spot.

"What is she doing Joey?" Dr. Robert said.

"She is holding out her hand for me to go with her," Joey replied.

"Go with her. We will stay with you," Dr. Robert whispered.

Joey walked in front of the group and stayed connected to Dr. Robert by the rope.

"Where are we going?" Sue asked.

"There is a tunnel in the basement that she wants him to go to. He has never gone, but he is going to try to today," Dr. Robert replied.

"It's OK Mom, I'm OK," Joey reassured Sue.

They continued to walk until they reached the entrance to the tunnel and Joey stopped.

"What's going on?" Dr. Robert asked.

"Her eyes are turning red," Joey said in a scared tone.

"Just stay here beside me. She can't hurt you," Dr. Robert reassured Joey.

"Her eyes are like fire. They're glowing," Joey said.

"Joey you don't have to do this. We can go home," Sue said.

"No, you have to find out what she wants, or the dreams will continue," Dr. Robert insisted.

"Her eyes are lighting up the tunnel, the flames are like a flashlight," Joey said with excitement.

"Keep following her Joey, stay close to her," Dr. Robert said.

"This is gross. It stinks and it's muddy," Sue moaned.

"Sue, we need to focus on Joey. We're coming to the well," Dr. Robert said as he could see the metal gate ahead.

"Sorry," Sue said quietly.

Joey continued to walk ahead of the group with Dr. Robert close behind. Joey reached the gate and could see the outline of the well just ahead of him. Suddenly, Joey came to a dramatic stop.

"What's wrong?" Dr. Robert asked.

"She is floating above the well," Joey said with concern.

"Keep walking toward the well, I have you tied to me and won't let you fall," Dr. Robert said.

"Are you sure he should do that?" Sue asked.

"I don't think she can hurt him," Rebecca said.

"What if he falls in the hole?" Sue said as Joey continued towards the well.

"I'm not going to let him fall," Dr. Robert reassured Sue.

Joey walked closer to the well and reached the stone edge and stopped.

Joey's arm became extended in front of him, and he started leaning back away from the well.

"She's pulling me!" Joey said frantically.

"Just hold on, I'll keep you out of the well," Dr. Robert said.

"What's inside the well?" Joey said in an excited voice.

"Joey, where is she?" Dr. Robert asked.

"She is on the other side of the well pulling me!" Joey said almost in a hysterical state.

"Move around the well, go to your right!" Dr. Robert yelled as he started pulling Joey around the side of the well.

"She's pulling me to the wall," Joey said as he continued to walk to the back wall. "She just went through it."

Dr. Robert, Rebecca and Sue gathered around Joey and begin examining the wall.

"What's this?" Rebecca said as she found a stone block that had a gap in the top of it.

"Let me see," Dr. Robert said moving to the block and putting his hand on top of the split block. "There is a handle."

"What's it for?" Sue asked.

"Everybody step back - I'm going to pull the handle," Dr. Robert said, bracing himself against the wall.

Dr. Robert began straining as he pulled the handle. After a few seconds of re-gripping and pulling the handle, the stone wall began to separate. It appeared to be a hidden door disguised as part of the wall that had not been opened for many years. Dr. Robert got the door partially opened and then stopped pulling the handle. Stepping toward the door, he began pushing the door until it released and flew open.

"What is it?" Rebecca asked.

"I can't see. Bring the lanterns over here," Dr. Robert said.

Sue handed Dr. Robert a lantern, and he stepped through the stone door.

"This is crazy! It's a room," Dr. Robert said.

"What is it?" Rebecca said, in an anxious tone.

"Come on in," Dr. Robert said stepping further into the room.

Dr. Robert noticed a power box against the wall and lifted the switch. Sparks flew from the box and slowly the room brightened, the lights faded off and on several time, before stabilizing in a well lit mode.

"What is this place?" Sue said, looking around at the room.

"This looks like an old operating room. But there is no way they brought patients all the way back here to operate on them," Rebecca said.

"Maybe the surgeries they were performing were not *routine* surgeries," Dr. Robert said.

"What kind of horrible place are you running here?" Sue asked.

"This happened way before my time. We didn't even know about this room, but I know who would," Rebecca said, looking at Dr. Robert.

"Michael Miller," Dr. Robert said.

"What did they do here?" Joey asked, showing his innocence.

"It looks like they did experimental operations on people and it was so bad they had to hide it," Dr. Robert explained. "Joey, is Sharon still here?"

"No, when you turned on the light she vanished," Joey replied.

"This must be what she wanted us to find," Dr. Robert said.

"I think we need to go back and have a talk with Michael," Rebecca said.

"I agree," Dr. Robert said.

Dr. Robert, Rebecca, Sue and Joey left the room and headed back out of the tunnel. Walking out no one said a word but reflected on their thoughts.

Reaching the exit and stepping out of the building, Sue made a loud sigh of relief.

"Are you OK," Rebecca asked.

"Yeah, just happy to be out of that place," Sue said.

"How are you doing Joey?" Rebecca asked.

"I feel better. I'm not scared of Sharon any more," Joey said.

Sue stepped over while Dr. Robert was untying the rope from Joey and hugged him. "I hope your bad dreams are over," Sue said.

"Rebecca, I can run Sue and Joey home, and when I come back, we can go talk to Michael," Dr. Robert said.

"I'll put all this stuff away," Rebecca said standing over the rope, lanterns and flashlights, "and meet you in my office when you get back."

"Sue, are you and Joey ready?" Dr. Robert asked.

"Sure, Joey, come on," Sue said as she began to walk toward the car.

Dr. Robert, Sue and Joey got into the car and started their trip back to Sue's car at Dr. Robert's office.

"What now?" Sue asked.

"My theory is that Sharon was trying to tell Joey what happened in the asylum. It appears as though some bad things happened," Dr. Robert said.

"What about Joey's dreams?" Sue asked.

"They should be over - unless there is something else she needs to tell him," Dr. Robert said.

"What about the other people I dream about?" Joey asked.

"I think the only reason you saw them was because they were using Sharon's energy to get you there," Dr. Robert said.

The conversation fell off until arriving at Sue's car.

"I appreciate all you have done for us, Dr. Robert," Sue said.

"I hope the bad dreams stop, and Joey, I hope you get some rest," Dr. Robert replied.

Sue and Joey got out of the car, and Dr. Robert headed back to the asylum.

Chapter Fifteen

Confronting Michael

"Rebecca, are you here?" Dr. Robert yelled into her office door.

"Yeah, I'll be right there," Rebecca yelled back.

Dr. Robert stepped back outside to wait for her to come out.

"Ready?" Rebecca said, as she stepped out the door.

"Waiting on you," Dr. Robert replied.

Dr. Robert and Rebecca got in the car and headed for Michael Miller's house.

"What are we going to ask him?" Rebecca asked.

"I don't know for sure. I figured we would just ask him about the room and let him talk," Dr. Robert said.

"Should we discuss how illegal it is to do experimental surgeries?" Rebecca asked.

"I think we should just hear what he has to say and then go from there," Dr. Robert said.

Pulling in front of Michael's house, Dr. Robert and Rebecca walked to the front door. Dr. Robert knocked on the door.

"You guys are becoming regulars," Sandy said, opening the door.

"I guess we are," Rebecca said, laughing.

"Is Michael available?" Dr. Robert asked.

"Yeah, come on in," Sandy said. "He's been acting really strange since you started coming around. You must be stirring his memory a little bit."

"He has a great memory, doesn't he?" Rebecca said.

"Yeah, I think he remembers everything," Sandy said.

"I hope so," Dr. Robert said.

"Michael, you have guests," Sandy said.

"I've been expecting them," Michael said.

Sandy walked out of the room and closed the door behind her.

Michael looked to make sure that Sandy left the room and asked, "Did you find it?"

"Find what?" Dr. Robert asked.

"Are you playing games with me?" Michael said, smiling.

"We found it. We found the room," Rebecca said.

"I knew when you mentioned Sharon's name that she must be coming back to make things right," Michael said.

"Tell us about the room," Dr. Robert said.

"I know I haven't been totally honest with you but I need to clear my conscience. What I told you about Elizabeth and Sharon is true, but how Sharon died is not actually true. When I took over the asylum, I was one of the leading neurosurgeons of my time, and I really thought I could help the patients. I worked for years at helping them and when Sharon was born, and became sick. I tried to help her. She was a teenager and out of control, hurting people and fighting all the time. I loved her so much that I just wanted to help her, but when I finally decided to try, it was too late. Her mind was gone. When I started the surgery everything was going fine. Then the anesthesia stopped working and she woke up. She started screaming things like, 'You will rot with me' and 'murderer' when she was awake. Her brain was exposed to the air, so she reached up and grabbed her own brain and pulled it out. It was the worst day of my life. The strange part about it was that when Sharon's heart stopped beating, black smoke came out of her head," Michael explained.

"What do you think it was?" Dr. Robert asked.

"I think it was the devil," Michael said.

"What happened after she died?" Rebecca asked.

"I stopped all experimental surgeries and closed off the tunnel. I realized that surgery could not fix mental illness," Michael said.

"You do know that experimental surgeries are illegal?" Dr. Robert asked.

"I know, that's why we had the well to dispose of the bodies," Michael replied.

"How many people do you think are in that well?" Rebecca asked.

"When I first started at the asylum it was my most active and most damaging year. In the first year there were probably over a hundred unsuccessful experiments. There were probably three times that many when I sealed the room," Michael confessed.

"How could you kill all those people and not care?" Rebecca asked horrified.

"Not care? I cared about those people more than their own families. They left them there and never came back. I was trying to give them a normal life," Michael replied.

"You know I have to report this. I took an oath, and so did you," Dr. Robert said.

"You can report me if you want, but it was different times back then," Michael said.

"Murder is murder, no matter what year it is," Rebecca said.

"You know, I've been waiting a long time to get that off my chest. I feel released from the burden of carrying that around inside of me," Michael said.

"I can't believe that you think that just because you confessed, it makes it better," Rebecca said in an aggravated tone.

After a minute of silence, Rebecca stood up and walked out of the room and out of the house.

"Michael, I'm leaving now. You understand that I am obligated by law to report what you just told me?" Dr. Robert asked.

"I understand, but can you do me one favor?" Michael asked.

"Depends on what it is?" Dr. Robert replied.

"Can you wait until tomorrow before you tell anyone? There is one more thing I want to do before the community finds out," Michael asked.

"It has been several years. I guess one more day won't hurt anything," Dr. Roberts said.

"Thank you for everything," Michael said as he reached up to shake Dr. Robert's hand.

Dr. Robert shook his hand and without another word walked out the door. He looked to the car and noticed Rebecca sitting in the car.

"Hey, what's up?" Dr. Robert asked as he climbed in the car.

"Nothing," Rebecca insisted.

"I know something is wrong because you're crying," Dr. Robert said.

"I sometimes get emotional because my brother is mentally impaired, and that could have been him," Rebecca explained.

"Listen, I talked to Michael and explained that I was going to the authorities. We are going to expose this injustice and make it right. He asked if we would wait until tomorrow, so he could make his peace with someone and I told him we would," Dr. Robert said.

"I don't have a problem with waiting until tomorrow. I just want to go home," Rebecca said as she lay back in the seat with her eyes closed.

"It has been an exhausting week, hasn't it?" Dr. Robert said.

Rebecca didn't answer him, and he drove her back to the asylum without breaking the silence. Pulling into the parking lot, Dr. Robert stopped the car and sat quietly for a minute.

"I'll come over in the morning, and we can figure out how we are going to handle this," Dr. Robert said.

"OK, I'll talk to you tomorrow," Rebecca said, getting out of the car.

Dr. Robert then drove home. The next morning, Dr. Robert awoke to the phone ringing.

"Hello," he said.

"Dr. Robert, I'm sorry to bother you so early, but this is Sue. I wanted you to know that Joey slept all night last night. He told me he didn't dream at all. I don't know how to thank you for giving me my nights back," Sue said.

"I'm so glad that Joey is resting peacefully now. Hopefully his bad dreams will not return," Dr. Robert said.

"Thank you again, Dr. Robert," Sue said.

"OK Sue, goodbye," Dr. Robert said, hanging up the phone.

Dr. Robert decided to go ahead and get a shower and prepare for the day. After getting out of the shower, he heard the phone ringing.

"Hello," he said, running into the bedroom.

"Hey, it's Rebecca," she said.

"Hey, what's up?" Dr. Robert asked.

"Haven't you heard? Haven't you seen the news?" Rebecca asked.

"Heard what?" Dr. Robert asked.

"Michael Miller died of a drug overdose last night," Rebecca said.

"Are you kidding me?" Dr. Robert said.

"No, I guess he asked his nurse to give him some time alone, and he took all of his sleeping pills," Rebecca said.

"Wow, I didn't see that coming," Dr. Robert said.

"What do you think we should do now?" Rebecca asked.

"I don't know, I wanted him to stand in front of the judge and explain what he had done," Dr. Robert said in a disappointed tone.

"I think that he needed to make his peace with God before he took the pills," Rebecca said.

"Do you think it will do any good to bring it out to the public now?" Dr. Robert asked.

"I think it's over. We don't have to bring any misery to the families. They'll never get closure since Michael is dead," Rebecca said.

"I agree," Dr. Robert said as he hung up the phone.

Chapter Sixteen

Confronting Michael Again

Dr. Robert gathered his file, and for the rest of the day, continued to produce a summary of the case. He looked through the file and realized that there was one drawing that could not be explained, the front entrance drawing. He thought that the best way to put total closure on the file was to meet with Joey one more time.

"Hello," Sue answered.

"Sue, this is Dr. Robert. I was wandering if I could have one more session with Joey?" He asked.

"Is something wrong, Dr. Robert?" Sue asked.

"No, I just wanted to ask him a couple follow-up questions," Dr. Robert said.

"I can bring him over tomorrow afternoon about one, if that's OK?" Sue said.

"Sure, see you tomorrow at one," Dr. Robert said.

Dr. Robert closed the file and decided to rest for the evening and try to forget about the stressful week that he had endured. Around six the next morning, Dr. Robert's phone rang.

"Hello," he said in a tired tone.

"Dr. Robert, this is Sue. Joey just had an awful dream, and I can't get him to calm down. He's been crying for the last hour, and I can't get him to stop," Sue said.

Dr. Robert could hear Joey screaming in the background and said, "Sue, can you see if he'll talk to me on the phone?"

Sue held the phone up to Joey's ear and said, "It's Dr. Robert."

"Joey, are you OK?" Dr. Robert asked.

"Yeah!" Joey screamed.

"Joey, you need to calm down I can't understand you," Dr. Robert said.

"OK," Joey said, catching his breath.

"Was it a dream?" Dr. Robert asked.

"Yeah," Joey answered.

"Was it Sharon?" Dr. Robert asked.

"No," Joey said.

"Who was it?" Dr. Robert asked.

"I don't know. It was an old man, and he told me that I needed to die," Joey replied.

"Do you know his name?" Dr. Robert asked.

"He said his name was Michael," Joey said.

Dr. Robert felt that Joey was now the reason there was a portal between Michael and the spirit world. Joey could manifest him in his dreams because Sharon opened the porthole for Joey to communicate with the spirits.

"Joey, settle down and I think we can solve this," Dr. Robert tried to reassure him even though he had no idea what he was going to do.

"OK, do you want me to come to your office," Joey said as if he would be protected there.

"Yes, that will be fine. Why don't you get dressed and eat some breakfast, and I will meet you there in a little bit," Dr. Robert said.

"OK," Joey said, handing the phone back to Sue.

"Thank you, Dr. Robert, what did you tell him?" Sue asked.

"I told him I would see him in about an hour. Can you bring him in?" Dr. Robert asked.

"If it keeps him from crying, I will," Sue said.

"OK, I'll see you in an hour," Dr. Robert said.

Close to an hour later, Sue and Joey showed up at Dr. Robert's office.

"Hey Joey, how are you feeling?" Dr. Robert asked.

"OK," Joey said.

"Joey, do you want to go to my office or sit out here?" Dr. Robert asked.

"Your office," Joey said.

Dr. Robert opened the door and let Joey lead them back to his office.

"OK Joey, tell me what happened last night," Dr. Robert said.

"I went back to the asylum, and there was an old man waiting for me at the entrance. As soon as I walked in the door, he put his hands on my neck and I couldn't breathe. It hurt really bad," Joey explained.

"Did he say anything to you?" Dr. Robert asked.

"He said I had to die so he could be free. What does that mean?" Joey asked.

"I don't know, but we will try to figure it out. How did you get loose?" Dr. Robert said.

"I fought him," Joey said.

"Joey, I think we have to go back to the asylum to face him," Dr. Robert said.

"No, I won't go!" Joey demanded.

"Joey, if this is the only way to put an end to the bad dreams, we should do it," Sue said.

"Joey, we will be there with you," Dr. Robert said.

"OK, but you better not let him hurt me," Joey said.

"Why don't you guys go out to the waiting room, and I will try to get a hold of Rebecca," Dr. Robert said.

Sue took Joey out to the waiting room and sat just outside the door.

Dr. Robert dialed Rebecca's number.

"Hello," Rebecca said in a sleepy tone.

"Rebecca, I'm sorry to call you so early but I have a problem," Dr. Robert said.

"What happened?" Rebecca said, perking up.

"Joey dreamed about Michael Miller last night, and he tried to kill him," Dr. Robert explained.

"How did he do that? He died?" Rebecca said.

"Joey went there in his dream, and Michael tried choking him to death," Dr. Robert said.

"What can I do?" Rebecca asked.

"I would like to bring Joey and his mom back to the asylum. I think if I can get him there, maybe we can talk to Michael through Joey and get him to leave him alone," Dr. Robert said.

"I'll be there as soon as I can," Rebecca said.

"I'll meet you at the front entrance in an hour," Dr. Robert said.

"OK, goodbye," Rebecca said, hanging up the phone.

Dr. Robert walked into the waiting room and asked Sue, "Are you ready to go?"

"I need to call my husband, Jim, but after that I will be ready," Sue said.

Sue called Jim and explained the plan, and then they headed to the asylum. Joey lay in the back seat of the car and struggled to stay awake to avoid dreaming.

"We're almost there Joey," Dr. Robert reassured Joey.

Dr. Robert pulled onto the asylum property a couple minutes later and pulled to the front entrance. Rebecca was walking through the parking lot and met them close to the front entrance.

"Good morning Rebecca," Dr. Robert said.

"Morning Dr. Robert, Sue, Joey," Rebecca said.

"We are here because Joey is having dreams about Michael, and we need to figure out how to stop him," Dr. Robert said.

"Do you have any ideas?" Rebecca asked.

"I hope that if Joey confronts him, we can find out what he wants and let him cross over to the other side," Dr. Robert said.

"What if it doesn't work?" Rebecca said.

"Well, Miss Positive, I don't really know," Dr. Robert said in a sarcastic tone.

"I'm sorry. I was just wondering if you had a back-up plan?" Rebecca said.

"Not really, we just have to figure out what he wants," Dr. Robert said.

"OK," Rebecca replied.

"Joey, are you ready?" Dr. Robert asked.

"Yeah," Joey replied.

"When we go in, ask him what he wants you to do," Dr. Robert said.

"OK," Joey said.

They walked to the front entrance. Dr. Robert grabbed the door handle and looked back at Joey. "If things start going bad, just run out of the building, or tell me and I will get you out of there."

"OK," Joey replied.

Dr. Robert slowly pulled the door open, looked inside and said, "I don't see anything."

Joey stepped up into the entrance and took a couple steps inside. Joey started screaming "What do you want? What do you want?"

"What's happening? What is he doing?" Dr. Robert started yelling trying to find out what Michael was saying.

Suddenly, Joey's voice became weak. He stood still and stared straight ahead.

"He's not breathing!" Sue screamed and grabbed Joey by the arms.

"Joey!" Dr. Robert grabbed him around the waist and ran out the door. He laid him on the ground and listened to see if he was breathing.

"Is he breathing?" Sue yelled frantically.

Dr. Robert grabbed him by the shoulders and shook him, "Breathe, Joey, breathe." He then bent down and pushed a breath of air into Joey's lungs.

"No!" Sue screamed and started crying.

"Look, he's breathing," Rebecca yelled.

Joey took a deep breath and then began breathing again on his own.

"Joey, are you OK?" Sue said trying to catch her breath from crying.

"Mom, what's wrong?" Joey said, as he looked up at his Mom.

Sue grabbed Joey and began hugging him.

"What did he say?" Dr. Robert asked.

"Leave him alone," Sue yelled at Dr. Robert.

"We have to know, or next time he might not be so lucky," Dr. Robert insisted.

"It's OK mom," Joey said in a weak voice. "He told me to set him free, but I don't know how."

"What did he mean 'set him free'?" Dr. Robert asked.

"I don't know...," Joey stopped talking. "Look," he said pointing at the window.

"What is it? What do you see?" Dr. Robert asked.

"It's Sharon. Look over there, its Elijah. There is someone in almost every window," Joey said.

"I don't see them. Where are they?" Sue said.

Joey got off the ground and walked to the entrance of the asylum and opened the door. Joey then took one step inside and yelled, "Stop!" holding his arm straight in front of him.

Michael was across the foyer and started running toward Joey when he yelled, "Help me Sharon."

Joey stood his ground as Michael drew nearer. Just before Michael got to him, Sharon appeared and knocked Michael back across the foyer.

Michael stood up and looked at Sharon, "Sharon, it's me, your father."

"You killed me! You're not my father," Sharon yelled as she charged toward Michael.

Michael grabbed Sharon and threw her to the floor. "You can't hurt me," he said.

Sharon sat on the floor, looking up at Michael, and with a smile on her face, she said, "You can beat me but you can't win against all of us."

"What? What are you talking about?" Michael asked.

In an instance, hundreds of spirits started walking from the hallways. Some had stitches in their heads, some had open wounds, and there were several with bandages still wrapped around their heads.

"What do you want? Who are you?" Michael started yelling as the crowd trapped him in the middle of them.

Joey stood in amazement, watching as Michael continued to scream as the crowd slowly attacked him. The crowd began moving toward the basement and headed for the tunnel. After the crowd left, Sharon moved over to Joey and looked him in the eyes. "Thank you," she said in a calming tone.

Joey smiled and nodded his head.

"Joey, what happened?" Dr. Robert asked.

"It's over, I don't want to talk about it," Joey replied as he turned and walked out the asylum door.